"You wore *that* to school?" Kate said to Cooper, sounding surprised.

"What?" Annie asked Kate. "She looks fine to me."

Kate nodded toward Cooper. "Look at her neck," she said quietly.

"Do I have a hickey?" Cooper asked, slapping her hand to her neck.

"No," Kate said. "It's your necklace."

Annie looked again and noticed the silver circle from the night before.

"You mean the pentacle?" Cooper asked. "What about it?"

"Everyone can see it," said Kate, as if that should be obvious to everyone.

"What's wrong with that?" Sasha said.

Kate sighed. "Don't you think that's asking for trouble?"

Follow the Circle:

circle of Three

BOOK
8

The five paths

isobel Bird

AVON BOOKS

An Imprint of HarperCollinsPublishers

For information address HarperCollins Children's Books,
a division of HarperCollins Publishers,
1350 Avenue of the Americas,
New York, NY 10019.

Library of Congress Catalog Card Number: 2001116349
ISBN 0-06-447298-1

First Avon edition, 2001

❖

Visit us on the World Wide Web!
www.harperteen.com

CHAPTER I

"Can you believe summer is actually over?" Sasha asked as the girls sat on the pier enjoying what they knew could very well be the last ice-cream cones of the season. The sky was blue and the sun shone brightly off the gently rolling ocean waves, but the breeze was noticeably cooler than it had been just a week before. They'd started wearing long sleeves again, although Sasha, Annie, and Kate were still in shorts. Cooper, of course, was dressed in jeans and her favorite black Doc Martens.

"It went by really fast," remarked Annie as she took a bite of her strawberry cone. "Why did it seem to last longer when we were kids?"

"Maybe because when we were kids all we did was play outside instead of worrying about cancer, breaking up with our boyfriends, and becoming a little too much like the goddesses we were invoking," Cooper suggested thoughtfully.

The others glared at her for a moment before breaking out in laughter. "Leave it to you to sum up the past two months so succinctly," said Kate, wiping traces of vanilla almond fudge off her lips.

"Well, it's all true," Cooper replied as she licked the edge of her mint chocolate chip cone just before it dripped on her leg.

She was right. All of those things *had* happened to them in the short time since their sophomore year had ended. In fact, a lot more had happened. First, Cooper had temporarily left their Wiccan group after a strange run-in with some out-of-control kids at a Midsummer ritual. Then, Kate's aunt had been diagnosed with cancer and they'd done a healing ritual for her, much to the concern of Kate's suspicious parents, who clearly were wondering just how involved their daughter was in Wicca. Most recently, Annie, who earlier in the summer had been saddened by the sudden death of one of the residents at the nursing home where she was volunteering, had undergone a weird transformation after invoking the goddess Freya during a full moon ceremony, causing all kinds of problems.

Although each of them had had her own issues to face, they'd all shared one particular ordeal during the summer: boyfriends. Sasha was still reeling from a terrible relationship with an ex from California, and Annie had gone on her first date and had her first kiss with Brian, a guy she'd met at a record store. Cooper and her boyfriend, T.J., had almost broken up after disagreeing about how public Cooper should be about her interest in witchcraft.

And Kate and her boyfriend, Tyler, were still trying to figure out exactly where they stood on that same subject, with Tyler urging Kate to be more open about her involvement in the Craft and Kate unsure of how to do that.

"I think it was easier when we just had to play hide-and-seek," said Kate.

"But not nearly as interesting," Annie added. "I wonder what will happen next."

"I hope nothing happens," Kate said. "I'd like it to be a stress-free junior year."

Nobody said anything for a few minutes as they all licked their cones and enjoyed the afternoon. Then Annie popped the tail end of her cone into her mouth, wiped her hands on her napkin, and proceeded to unzip her backpack. She pulled out a sheaf of papers.

"Here," she said, handing one piece to each of them. "As promised, I collated all of our schedules and put them on one page so we can see where everybody will be and when."

They'd received their schedules a couple of weeks earlier. Although they'd each been excited to see that they'd gotten into classes they'd wanted, there had also been some unpleasant surprises. Looking at all of their daily routines combined on one page, they were reminded that not everything had come out the way they'd hoped.

"Algebra at eight in the morning," Cooper said grimly. "I could barely do it at eleven in the morning last year. I'm doomed."

"At least you don't have to take gym at the end of the day," Kate said.

"Nobody told you to play basketball, jockette," replied Cooper jokingly. "And this year you'll be on the varsity team."

"*If* I decide to play," Kate said. "I still haven't made up my mind."

"Your parents will flip if you don't," said Annie.

Kate nodded. "I know," she said. "But I'm not sure I'm as into it as I used to be. Besides, Tara and Jessica will be on the team, and that might be weird."

They were all silent as they thought about what Kate had said. Tara and Jessica were two of her former best friends. Things had been up and down between them ever since Kate had stopped hanging around with them and Sherrie Adams, the other member of their once-inseparable group. The situation had been further strained when Sherrie had spread a vicious rumor about Tara after she'd helped Kate and her friends embarrass Sherrie in public. And when Annie slapped Sherrie in front of Jessica a few weeks before the end of the summer, it had seemed to sever the last ties between Sherrie and the girls who had once hung on her every word.

Kate, Cooper, and Annie were all happy to see Sherrie get her comeuppance, but they didn't know what might happen next. Sherrie wasn't one to take defeat quietly, and they all suspected that she might

4

try to cause trouble for them if she could. Annie in particular was apprehensive about seeing Sherrie again. And although Tara and Jessica appeared to have given up on Sherrie, none of the girls knew where they stood with the two of them now.

"You guys worry too much," Sasha said, breaking the silence. "Look at the bright side—we all have lunch together."

"Not me," Kate said glumly, correcting her. "I have lunch fifth period. You guys have it sixth. The only class we all have together is history, and that's hardly going to be fun, especially since we don't have Mr. Draper this year. We have Mrs. Greeley."

They all groaned at that. Where Mr. Draper was young and had a sense of humor, students joked that Mrs. Greeley had been teaching at Beecher Falls High School since the Ice Age and had a personality to match. The girls weren't looking forward to a year of facing her frosty personality on a daily basis.

"Hey," Annie said lightly. "At least we all got the special stuff we wanted. I got on the school paper, Cooper got into the creative writing class, and Sasha is in drama club. Plus, Kate, Sasha, and I are all in driver's ed together."

"Okay," Kate said. "So there's one good thing."

"And you and I have French together third period," Cooper reminded her. "We can conjugate together."

Kate smiled. *"Mais oui,"* she said.

"And I have fifth period study time," Annie

pointed out. "I'm sure I can sneak into the caf for lunch with you from time to time."

"What?" Cooper said, feigning shock. "Annie Crandall skipping a study period? Am I hearing you right?"

Annie flipped her hair and gave Cooper a look. "Not everything went back to normal when I asked Freya to back off," she said, referring to her recent experience with aspecting the assertive goddess.

"What's Brian's schedule like?" Sasha asked Annie. "Will you two have any classes together?"

Annie shook her head. "He's a senior," she explained. "But we'll see a lot of each other anyway. At least I hope we will. We're both going to be really busy."

One of the things Annie had feared about giving up the aspects of Freya's personality that she'd taken on after her invocation ritual was that Brian wouldn't be interested in her anymore. But she'd discovered that she really *had* changed during her experience. She was more confident and more out-going. She'd learned a lot about herself, and it had had a big effect on her. She and Brian were still going out, and he hadn't seemed to notice anything different about her at all. She didn't know where things would go with them, but she was having a good time for now and that was what mattered.

"T.J. is in our history class, too," Cooper told her friends. "I think that's about the only real class we have together, which is fine with me. Too much togetherness would make me nuts."

"Ever the romantic," Sasha teased.

"So what should we do on our last night of freedom?" Kate asked.

"Movie?" suggested Annie.

"Dinner?" Sasha offered.

"New moon ritual?" proposed Cooper.

"It is a new moon, isn't it?" Annie said. "What a good time to be starting a new school year."

"How about all three, then?" Kate said. "We can rent a video, hang out at Annie's, and do a little ritual. You know, something to get things started off on the right foot."

"Sounds good to me," Annie said.

"I'm in," confirmed Sasha.

"Sure," agreed Cooper. "But what kind of ritual should we do?"

"Technically, I'm not supposed to do rituals," Sasha reminded them. "Remember?"

Although Sasha lived with one of the coven members who taught the weekly Wicca study group that Cooper, Annie, and Kate were a part of, Sasha herself wasn't in the group. She came to some of the coven's open rituals, but she wasn't officially a student yet. All the problems she had spent her life running from had crashed down on her when the rest of them had undergone the dedication ceremony marking the beginning of their year and a day of studying witchcraft, and it had been decided that she should wait until the next year's ceremony before starting on her journey toward deciding if she wanted to be initiated as a witch.

"This won't be a big-deal ritual," Kate said. "I'm thinking of something really simple. Maybe we could each bring something to bless. You know, like a good luck charm for the year."

"Good thinking," Annie said. "We can light a little fire in the cauldron and pass things through it or something."

Kate looked at Cooper and Sasha. "Sound okay?" she asked.

The others nodded.

"Good," Kate said. "Cooper, you're in charge of the video. Annie, you're the cauldron wrangler and ritual designer. Sasha and I will be on food detail. Any requests?"

"What movie do we want to see?" asked Cooper.

"Something spooky," Sasha said.

"Something Leonardo DiCaprio—free," Annie added.

"Nothing with subtitles," Kate stated firmly.

"Got it," Cooper said. "I think I know just the thing."

"How about food?" said Sasha.

"No meat for me," Cooper replied.

"No pizza or Chinese," Annie told them. "We've done those to death."

"We'll surprise you, then," Kate said. "Okay, we all have our assignments. I say we break up and meet at Annie's at seven. Don't forget to bring your objects for blessing."

They walked to the end of the pier and then went their separate ways. But four hours later they were all together again, this time in Annie's big bedroom at the top of her house.

"The entertainment has arrived," Cooper had announced as she walked in swinging a bag from the video store. Kate and Cooper were already there, several bags of food sitting on the floor.

Cooper sniffed the air. "I smell lemongrass," she said. "Could we be having Thai this evening?"

"You got it," Kate answered as she opened one of the bags. "Pad thai for everyone."

"Plus some pad prighking, green curry with tofu, and tom yum," continued Sasha. "So what's the movie?"

"Ah," Cooper replied, pulling a tape out of the bag. "I have chosen the perfect film. Creepy yet romantic. No subtitles or Leonardo. Plus, it has some witchy stuff in it. Not to mention Johnny Depp, which elevates it to instant classic."

"*Sleepy Hollow!*" Annie, Kate, and Sasha said in unison.

"None other," Cooper confirmed as she tossed the video onto Annie's bed. "So what's the order for the evening?"

"I think dinner, ritual, and then movie," Annie said. "All in favor?"

The others answered her by sitting down and

opening the containers of food. Serving spoons flashed and hands reached across one another, and soon every plate was piled with noodles, rice, and spicy green beans, and the tom yum was splashing in the little bowls Annie had brought up from the kitchen to hold the soup.

"There's nothing like chili paste to wake you up," Cooper said, taking a big bite of the pad prighking with its spicy orange sauce coating the crisp beans.

The others murmured their agreement, their mouths too full to talk. For a while the only sound in the room was that of everyone chewing and making noises of contentment. When the last noodle was slurped up and the last bit of tofu was gone, they all leaned back and sighed happily.

"Ritual time," Annie said. "Can you guys clear this stuff up while I get ready?"

The others nodded and got to work. They carried the empty containers downstairs to the garbage and put the dishes they'd used in the kitchen sink. When they came back they saw that Annie had put the three-legged cauldron in the center of the room and lit a circle of candles around it.

"All set," Annie said. "Let's fire this baby up."

The four of them stood around the cauldron inside the circle of candles. Annie held out one hand to Sasha and one to Kate, who were on either side of her. They in turn took Cooper's hands, so that they were all linked together.

"We're going to cast the circle in a different way tonight," Annie informed them. "I want to try something new. Since there are four of us I want us each to take a different direction. I'll be east, Sasha will be south, Cooper will be west, and Kate will be north. I want us each to think about our direction, the element it represents, and the qualities associated with it. Then we're going to go around the circle, each of us saying a word that comes to mind when we think about our direction. We'll go around a couple of times. Try to imagine a circle of light forming as we do it."

She paused for a moment as they all thought about the elements they were representing. Then she said in a clear voice, "Inspiration."

"Passion," Sasha said, following her.

"Mystery," said Cooper.

"Strength," Kate said, finishing the first round.

They continued, each of them saying a word. As they did the words formed a kind of chant, their voices rising and falling as they thought of different things to say. "Flying, dancing, diving, planting, wind, fire, waves, stone," they said, the words combining to create a rhythm. "Bird, dragon, whale, bear, birth, life, sleep, death."

After they'd gone around several times Annie said, "The circle is cast." She let go of Sasha's and Kate's hands and motioned for them all to sit down. Then she took a bottle of clear liquid, opened it, and poured the liquid into the cauldron. Striking a

11

match, she dropped it in as well, and the cauldron sprang to life with bright flames that burned without smoke.

"Rubbing alcohol," she said as the others looked at the fire. "A little trick I picked up in chemistry class."

"Very nice," Cooper said.

"Did you all bring something to bless in the sacred fire?" Annie asked.

The others rummaged around in their pockets and took out the things they'd brought. They held them in their hands as Annie spoke.

"The new moon is a time for new beginnings," she said. "Tomorrow we start a new year at school. We each want to accomplish different things this year. The fire in the cauldron represents the fires of inspiration, courage, and passion. By passing our sacred objects through the fire and stating what we hope they will bring to us as we start this new journey, we're using the magic within ourselves to make what we want to happen come true."

She held up her object. It was a pen, an old-fashioned silver one. "This belonged to my father," she said. "It was one of the few things that survived the fire. He used it to write in his journal. One of the things I want to do this year is write for the school paper. This pen represents that, and I hope that when I write I will write with honesty and that my words will help people see the truth."

She passed the pen slowly through the flames

that jumped up from the cauldron. They wrapped around the sides, coating the pen in fire, before she drew it clear of them.

Kate went next, holding up her object for everyone to see. It was a ring. "This is a ring that Tyler gave me about a month after we started dating," she explained. "I haven't really worn it much lately because of what's been going on between him and me. It's a Celtic knot design, and to me it represents how everything is connected. I know that there are a lot of things in my life that need to be connected, and I hope that wearing this ring again will remind me of that."

She passed the ring quickly through the flames, adding, "I hope that the strength of this fire will fill me and help me to do what I need to do."

When Kate was finished Sasha knelt in front of the fire. "This might be a little weird," she said. She held up a key. "This is the key to the front door of our house. I've never really had a key to my own house before. This is the first time I've ever really felt at home anywhere. So it means a lot to me. I want to bless it because I really want this to work."

She put the end of the key into the flames for a few seconds, looking at the fire with a peaceful expression. When she pulled the key out again, she held it tightly in her hand.

"It's so warm," she said, laughing.

"My turn," Cooper said. She held out her palm. On it lay something small and round and silver; it was attached to a black cord. It was a circle with a five-pointed star inside it. The lines forming the points of the star were connected, and it had one corner pointing up, two corners pointing to the sides, and two corners pointing down.

"This is a pentacle I got at Crones' Circle," Cooper announced. "Actually, I bought it today right before I went to the video store. I've been looking at it for a couple of weeks now, and when Kate said we should each bring a talisman of some kind I figured the time was right to buy it. As you all know, the pentacle is one of the strongest symbols of the Craft. This one symbolizes my commitment to studying Wicca. And I bought it at the store where we all study, which seemed even more appropriate."

She dangled the pentacle from its cord and held it in the fire. "Blessing this with fire is also symbolic for me," she said. "It feels like I've been jumping into fires a lot since I started all of this, and every time it's made me stronger. I hope this one does the same thing."

She removed the pentacle from the fire and put it around her neck, knotting the cord in the back. It hung just beneath the hollow of her throat, glinting against her pale skin.

"Okay," Cooper said. "Ritual's over. Now let's open this circle and get to Johnny Depp!"

CHAPTER 2

Kate fumbled with the combination lock on her new locker. She kept missing the second number, and she was getting annoyed at having to start over every time she screwed up.

"Why can't we just have our old lockers?" she said irritably.

"Because then the new freshmen wouldn't have any," said Annie reasonably. "Every year we all move up a little. Last year's seniors leave to make way for last year's juniors. We move up to make room for the old freshmen. And the newbies come in from junior high and take *their* places. It's like shark teeth."

"Like what?" asked Kate, looking at the piece of paper in her hand and trying her combination again.

"Shark teeth," Annie repeated. "Sharks' teeth are constantly falling out and being replaced. It's like they're on a conveyer belt. The old ones are pushed forward as the new ones come in behind them. I saw it on the Discovery Channel."

"Why can't you watch Buffy like every other teenage girl?" Kate said, finally getting her locker to open and sticking some notebooks and her lunch inside it.

"Hey, kids," said Cooper, walking up to them with Sasha. "Happy first day back in hell."

"Hey," Annie said back, distracted by trying to figure out what to take with her and what to leave in her backpack.

"You wore *that* to school?" Kate said, sounding surprised.

Annie looked up at Cooper. She was dressed in jeans and a Kittie T-shirt featuring the cover of the band's CD and the words MAKE ME PURR scrawled across it. Her hair, which was always changing color, had been returned to some semblance of her normal blondish brown color and was sticking up in a controlled mess like it usually was.

"What?" Annie asked Kate. "She looks fine to me."

Kate nodded toward Cooper. "Look at her neck," she said quietly.

"Do I have a hickey?" Cooper asked, slapping her hand to her neck.

"No," Kate said. "It's your necklace."

Annie looked again and noticed the silver circle from the night before.

"You mean the pentacle?" Cooper asked. "What about it?"

"Everyone can see it," said Kate, as if that should be obvious to everyone.

"What's wrong with that?" Sasha said.

Kate sighed. "Don't you think that's asking for trouble?"

Cooper looked perplexed. "Not really," she said. "Anyway, I thought the whole point of having a talisman was to have it on you. You're wearing your ring."

"Yes," Kate said. "But my ring isn't quite so obvious. And I'm sure Annie and Sasha have theirs in their pockets or backpacks or somewhere discreet. Yours is right out there in the open."

Cooper rolled her eyes. "I really don't think anyone is going to notice," she said. "They're all too busy worrying about everyone else looking at *them*. Besides, how many people here are going to know what this is?"

"Cooper's right, Kate," Annie told her friend. "I don't think anyone will even notice it."

"Besides," Cooper said, "they'll be too busy wondering what happened to Annie."

Annie looked down at her outfit. She was wearing a gray skirt and a lavender sweater with a white T-shirt under it. Her hair hung loose about her shoulders, and she had put on a little makeup. An improved sense of style was something else she'd retained from her time with Freya. She'd gotten used to it, and it hadn't occurred to her that the other students hadn't seen the new her yet.

"I still think it's a bad idea," Kate said. "But whatever."

17

"What's first on the agenda for everyone today?" Sasha asked.

"Algebra," Cooper said, looking at her schedule. "The perfect way to start the school year."

"English," Kate replied.

"Same here," Sasha said.

"I've got Spanish," Annie answered.

"I told you to take French," Kate chided her. "Cooper and I have that third period."

"I couldn't fit it in and still take calculus," said Annie.

"Like anyone would *want* to take calculus," Cooper retorted as they started to walk down the hall. "I guess we'll see you second period, then, in Greeley's lair."

They split up, with Sasha and Kate heading upstairs to Mr. Tharpe's English class while Annie went to Ms. Lopez's room for Spanish and Cooper headed to Mr. Niemark's room for yet another year of mathematic excitement. Cooper's room came first in the hall, so Annie found herself walking alone to her class.

She was actually looking forward to Spanish. She'd taken it in junior high but had skipped it the previous two years. Now she wanted to get back into it. There were a couple of Spanish-speaking residents at Shady Hills, where she volunteered a few afternoons a week, and she thought it would be nice to speak to them in their own language. Plus, it would look good on her college applications. She'd had to test to get into this third-year class after not taking it for so long, and she'd been relieved to have passed fairly easily. Still, she knew she had a lot of work to do.

She stepped into the class and almost ran out of the room. There were a couple of other students finding their seats and chatting with one another. They all seemed pretty excited to be back with their friends. But sitting in the back row, a scowl on her face, was Sherrie Adams.

What is she doing here? Annie thought as she looked at Sherrie. She'd been trying to not think about running into Sherrie, but now she had not only run into her but had to be in the same class with her. *So much for getting off to a good start*, she thought miserably.

She didn't know what to do. The last time she'd seen Sherrie had been in a clothing store, where Annie had slapped Sherrie after she had made a remark about Annie's parents. It had been a wonderful feeling at the time, but now Annie just felt sick. She knew Sherrie wouldn't ignore what had happened. She also knew from something Jessica—who had witnessed the incident—had said that Sherrie had been stewing about it ever since it happened. Who knew what horrible plan she had come up with for getting back at Annie.

Annie stood in the doorway, unable to move. She felt both angry and stupid. *Freya would have known what to do*, she thought. After all, it had been Freya who had slapped Sherrie. Well, not entirely Freya.

Annie had wanted to slap Sherrie. But she never would have done it without Freya's influence. Now, without the goddess around to help her out, she was on her own, and she had no idea how to act.

Then she realized that Sherrie wasn't even looking at her. She sat in her chair, an unpleasant look plastered on her face as she stared straight ahead. It was as if she hadn't even seen Annie in the doorway. But Annie knew that wasn't possible. Of all people, Sherrie would be the one to be keeping an eye on who was coming into the class, if only to try to get the cutest guy to sit by her. But there she sat, seemingly oblivious to the fact that the person who had humiliated her a few weeks before was now only fifteen feet away.

Finally, after what seemed like an eternity, Annie was able to move. She walked into the class-room and sat down as far from Sherrie as she could get, in the seat closest to the door. She opened her notebook and pretended to be looking at some-thing while she tried to sneak glances in Sherrie's direction to see if the other girl was looking at her. But every time she looked, Sherrie was sitting there with the same vacant stare and hostile expression.

The bell rang and Ms. Lopez came in, shutting the door behind her. Annie was relieved to have class begin, as it meant that she could concentrate on what the teacher was saying and try to forget all about Sherrie. But as hard as she tried she couldn't ignore the fact that the person who hated her more than anyone else in the world was sitting behind her.

When the bell rang forty-five minutes later Annie gathered up her books and stood up. She wanted to leave the room before Sherrie did. But when she turned to go she found that Sherrie was already ahead of her, pushing past several other students to get into the hallway.

Annie walked out after her, watching as Sherrie strode quickly away down the hall. It was almost as if she wanted to get away from Annie. *That's weird*, Annie thought as she walked to her next class. *Usually, Sherrie's the one coming after people, not running away from them.* She knew she should be thrilled that she and Sherrie hadn't had a run-in. But in some ways that would have been better than not knowing what Sherrie was thinking or planning. This way she had no idea what was going on in Sherrie's head, and that worried her more than having to stand up to her did.

She made it to Mrs. Greeley's class with a few minutes to spare. Kate, Cooper, and Sasha were already there, and they had saved her a seat. T.J. was in the class as well, and he sat next to Cooper. The five of them formed a little group, and they talked while they waited for class to begin.

"How'd Spanish go?" Cooper asked Annie.

"Fine," Annie answered. "Except that Sherrie is in my class."

Her friends' eyes went wide. They all knew about the slapping incident, although none of them had witnessed it firsthand.

"And?" Kate asked impatiently.

Annie started to answer, but just then Mrs. Greeley entered the room, shutting the door with such a bang that everyone jumped.

"Now that I have your attention," she said in her nasal voice, "I'd like you all to listen closely. I know many of you think that class time is an opportunity to hang out with your friends and catch up on all the latest gossip. Let me disabuse you of that notion. You are here to learn about American history. To make that easier for you I would like you to sit in alphabetical order, beginning with Miss Aarons."

Mrs. Greeley pointed to the first desk in the first row along the windows. Emily Aarons got up from a seat next to her friends and walked over to it. She was followed by Jeremy Bowers and Savannah Butler as Mrs. Greeley read off their names and pointed to their assigned seats.

Annie was in the fifth seat, almost in the back of the room. Her friends were scattered throughout the class, depending on their last names. T.J., being a McAllister, happened to be directly in front of Kate, a Morgan, but Cooper and Sasha were by themselves several rows apart. All Annie could do was look at them all and smile helplessly.

Things were definitely not getting off to a good start. The Sherrie thing had unsettled her, and now in the one class they all had together she and her friends couldn't even sit by one another. If this was how all her classes were going to go, it was going to be a *very* long year.

Annie barely listened as Mrs. Greeley lectured them about the early American colonies. She knew that it was all in their textbook anyway. Mrs. Greeley was infamous for simply reading her lectures straight out of the text. You didn't even have to take notes in her class; you simply had to memorize whatever the book said and repeat it on her tests.

Things improved a little in Annie's next class, calculus. She was good with numbers, which was why her friends had to suffer through a second year of algebra while she got to sit in with the seniors. Then, in fourth period, she was reunited with Kate and Sasha, this time for driver's ed. The three of them were excited about taking the class. Cooper already had her license, as well as a car, but the rest of them still had only their learner's permits.

Their instructor was Mr. Caffrey, who also taught gym. He was a large, easygoing man, and Annie knew the class was going to be fun. The first day was spent going over the first chapter in the driving manuals issued by the state. Then they were split into groups for actual driving practice, which would begin in a couple of weeks. Annie and her friends managed to get into the same group, which brightened her outlook considerably as she headed off to the rest of her classes.

She reconvened with Sasha and Cooper at lunch. They were sitting at their usual table when Annie entered.

"It's nice to see that some things never change," Annie remarked as she pulled out a chair and sat down. "It feels like we were just sitting here last week."

"I just wish Kate were here," Sasha said. "I feel bad for her having to eat by herself."

"Don't look now, Crandall, but your man is coming this way," Cooper said.

Annie looked around and saw Brian headed for their table. When he reached it he smiled. "Mind if I crash your party?" he asked.

"Not at all," Annie replied, amazed that she could sound so cool when she was really thrilled to have Brian sit with her. She knew that people were looking at them and wondering who the new guy was and why he was sitting with Annie. *Let them wonder*, she thought happily.

"How's the first day going?" Cooper asked Brian.

Brian shrugged. "Better now," he said. "But it's been okay. Nothing too bad, nothing too exciting. How about you guys?"

Annie looked at her friends. She really wanted to talk to them about Sherrie, but with Brian there she couldn't. He didn't know about the slapping incident, and she didn't want him to know. What would he think of her if he found out? She certainly couldn't tell him that she'd been under the influence of a goddess she'd invoked. She was waiting until they knew each other a little better before bringing up the subject of Wicca.

"Driver's ed was cool," Sasha told him, saving Annie from having to come up with something to say. "Of course, it will be cooler when we're actually *in* a car, but hey."

The rest of lunch was filled with conversation about their various classes. Annie was happy that Brian was fitting in with her friends so well. So far things were going smoothly, and she wanted to keep it that way. Then, Cooper stood up to go get another drink.

"What's that symbol?" Brian asked Cooper, pointing to the pentacle that was swinging from its cord.

"Oh," Cooper said, looking at Annie. "It's just a good luck charm."

Brian looked more closely. "It looks familiar."

"It's a really old symbol," Sasha told him. "You've probably seen it on a lot of things."

"I know what it is," Brian said, ignoring her. "It was on a CD that came into the store the other day. One of those goth metal bands or something. Maybe Marilyn Manson or White Zombie—one of those freaky groups. Are you into them?"

"No," Cooper said simply as she walked away.

"It's just a good luck charm," Annie repeated, hoping Brian would buy the story and leave it at that. She was surprised that he'd even noticed the pentacle. Even she had forgotten about it until he'd said something.

By the time Cooper returned Brian *had* forgotten about it, or had at least lost interest in the subject.

He didn't mention it again for the rest of the period, and when it was time to go to their next classes the only thing he seemed interested in was walking with Annie.

She had two more classes before the one period she really wanted to get to. The first was advanced chemistry with her teacher from the previous year, Ms. Blackwood. Then she had English with Mr. Tharpe before the last period of the day rolled around. As she walked to her final destination she felt herself growing excited.

She'd always thought about working on the school paper, the *Sentinel*. But while she was good with numbers and scientific formulas, words had never been especially easy for her. It wasn't until she'd started creating her own spells and circle-casting rituals that she'd become more comfortable with writing and using language. Now she felt ready to try something she'd wanted to do but was sort of afraid of.

She walked into Mr. Barrows's room. He was the paper's adviser, as well as the school's speech teacher. Annie had never taken a class with him, so she had no idea what to expect. There were several other students already in the room, some of whom she knew and others she didn't. Many of them were seniors, with a few juniors and underclassmen thrown in.

"Welcome," Mr. Barrows said, smiling at Annie. He was a tall man, in his mid-thirties, with short brown hair and round glasses. He was wearing a blue shirt with a yellow tie, and his sleeves were rolled up almost to the elbow. *He looks like an ad for J. Crew,* Annie thought as she smiled back.

"Why don't we all form a circle with our chairs," Mr. Barrows suggested.

People moved around, getting their seats into a roughly circular shape. Annie took a chair directly across from Mr. Barrows and sat down.

"Some of you I know from last year," Mr. Barrows began. "Some of you are new. For those of you who haven't worked on the paper before, the way this works is that you all make it happen. I'm here to help out, but the real work is yours. We always have an editor and an assistant editor. They work together to assign stories and decide what goes in the paper. We also have a team that works on design and layout. Can I have a show of hands for those who are interested in design?"

A number of students raised their hands. Mr. Barrows looked around at them and nodded. "Good," he said. "We should have no problem there. I assume, then, that the rest of you want to be on the writing end. As I said, we start off by choosing our editor and assistant editor. Normally the editor is a senior and the assistant editor is a junior. That way the assistant learns how things work and can take over the following year. Last year our assistant editor was Joel Nevins. Joel, I'm assuming you'll be taking the editor's hat this year?"

"You bet," replied Joel, a short, pleasant-looking

guy sitting a few seats away from Annie. "I didn't do all the grunt work last year for nothing."

Everyone laughed, including Mr. Barrows. "Joel's not entirely kidding," he said. "The assistant editor's job is often a thankless one. But it's a great way to learn about putting a newspaper together. Are there any volunteers this year?"

Annie waited for people to raise their hands. She was sure that everyone would want the assistant editor's job. But to her surprise no hands went up. Mr. Barrows looked around the circle expectantly.

"Come on," he said encouragingly. "Someone must want to do this. How about you?"

He was looking at a girl to Annie's right. She shook her head. "I'm more interested in reporting and writing," she said. "I'm not good at the organizational stuff."

Mr. Barrows sighed, pretending to be upset. "You writers are never organized," he said. "Doesn't *someone* in this group have a logical bone in their body?"

I do, Annie thought suddenly. But there was no way she could be the assistant editor. She'd never even worked on a paper before. She didn't know the first thing about it.

You didn't know anything about witchcraft before you tried it either, she reminded herself.

Before she knew what she was doing she had raised her hand. Mr. Barrows looked at her and smiled. "Ah," he said. "A willing victim."

CHAPTER 3

"Want some company?"

Kate looked up from her lunch to see Jessica and Tara standing next to her table. For a moment she was so shocked she didn't know what to say.

"If you'd rather be alone—" Jessica started to say.

"No!" said Kate, interrupting her. "Sit down. Please."

Tara and Jessica pulled out chairs and sat. Tara opened her bag and took out a sandwich, while Jessica opened a container of pasta salad. As they did, Kate looked around the cafeteria. Just as she'd thought, Sherrie was there. She was sitting at the table she usually shared with her friends, but now she was sitting all by herself, chewing on some carrot sticks as if she always ate lunch alone.

"Aren't you guys going to sit with Sherrie?" she asked hesitantly. When she'd walked into the cafeteria the day before she had been dismayed to see that not only didn't she have the same lunch period as her friends did but that she had to share her forty-five minutes with Sherrie.

"Does it *look* like we're going to sit with Sherrie?" Jessica asked her.

"You know what I mean," replied Kate. "Isn't she going to freak if she sees you eating with me?"

"We're big girls now," Tara told her. "We can sit wherever we want to."

"Translation: We told Sherrie to take a hike," said Jessica, tucking her long blond hair behind her ear.

"Really?" Kate exclaimed, not sure she believed it.

"After what she did to me I knew I would never trust her again," Tara explained.

"And let's just say that Sherrie wasn't the only one who was woken up by Annie's slap," Jessica added. "Seeing how Sherrie acted that day was the last straw for me."

"So what did you tell her?" Kate asked, curious to hear how they had told Sherrie the news.

Jessica and Tara looked at each other. Then Jessica grimaced. "We sort of didn't say anything," she said. "Tara was already not speaking to her. I just stopped returning her calls. I think she got the message when I didn't wait for her to walk to school yesterday."

"That explains the weird mood," said Kate thoughtfully.

"Weird mood?" Tara echoed.

Kate nodded. "Annie and Sherrie are in the same Spanish class," she explained. "Annie was expecting some big showdown when Sherrie saw her, but nothing happened. She said it was like Sherrie didn't even know she was in the same room."

"Annie really shocked her," said Jessica. "No one has ever stood up to Sherrie like that. I don't think she's quite over it."

"Either that or she's planning something *really* nasty," said Tara. "Look at what she did to me."

"How *are* things with Ali?" Kate asked, referring to the guy Tara had been seeing before Sherrie started a rumor that the two of them had slept together when they hadn't.

"We decided to be just friends," Tara answered. "But it wasn't because of those rumors Sherrie started about us. Like you predicted, people forgot about that pretty quickly. We hung out a lot over the summer and had a good time, and I really like him, but I don't really want anything full-time right now."

"Listen to you," Kate said, grinning. "One boyfriend and you're Miss Hot Stuff."

Tara laughed, her freckled Irish complexion turning pink. "I just grew up a little," she said. "I don't need a boyfriend to make me happy."

There was a pause in the conversation as the three of them ate. Then Kate said, "I really missed you guys."

"Same here," said Jessica. "I can't believe we let Sherrie keep us apart like we did."

"It's like she had some evil spell over us or something," said Tara.

"And she said you guys were the ones who were

witches," added Jessica, laughing.

"She said what?" asked Kate.

"Oh, it's just something Sherrie said," Jessica said. "She said that you, Cooper, and Annie reminded her of the three witch sisters from *Macbeth*. I didn't even know she knew who Shakespeare was, let alone read him. Then I realized that she was reading it in English last year. She thought she was so clever dropping literary references."

Kate laughed but didn't say anything. It wasn't the first time Sherrie had made witch references when speaking about Kate, Cooper, and Annie. Kate had always managed to deflect them, but it bothered her that Sherrie was hitting so close to home, especially when there was really no way for her to know what Kate and her friends were up to. It was almost like she was picking up on something that other people couldn't see.

Forget about it, Kate told herself. *No one is paying any attention to Sherrie now anyway.* That at least seemed to be true. Jessica and Tara were sitting with *her* again, not with Sherrie. It was like Kate had finally won them over from the dark side or something. Thinking about that made her feel good.

"So fill us in on what we missed while we were away," Jessica said. "Who's that cute guy I saw you with at the restaurant?"

"Oh, that's Tyler," answered Kate. She'd momentarily forgotten about Jessica's waitressing job. But of course Jessica would wonder who Tyler was after seeing them together.

"He's majorly cute," Jessica said. "I take it you're going out?"

"Sort of," Kate told her. This part was going to be hard to explain, she realized. She couldn't really tell Jessica and Tara that she and Tyler were on a break from their relationship because she was trying to figure out how to tell her family that she was involved in the Craft. That would mean telling *them* that she was involved in it, and she wasn't ready to do that.

"How can he sort of be your boyfriend?" said Tara, opening a bag of chips and munching on one.

Kate sighed. "We're just going through a rough spot right now," she said. She hated not being able to tell them the truth, especially now that they seemed to be her friends again, but she just couldn't. They'd had enough trouble understanding her splits from Sherrie and from her ex-boyfriend, Scott. While eventually they'd come around, she knew that telling them she was in a Wicca study group might shatter the tentative bond that was re-forming between them.

"Well, I hope you work it out," Jessica told her. "He seemed nice."

Kate smiled. *I hope we do, too*, she thought sadly.

"You're going to play on the team this year, right?" asked Tara. "We're finally on the varsity squad. And *this* year I'm keeping my grades up so I don't get benched like I did last season."

Kate had been thinking a lot about basketball.

She really loved playing. It was something she was good at, and it made her feel confident about herself. Moving down the court with the ball in her hands and then going up for a basket gave her a feeling she'd only ever experienced when doing a really good ritual. It was like she was filled with energy and power and could do anything she wanted to.

She, Jessica, and Tara had played together since junior high. Last year things had been rough because Kate had stopped hanging around with them. She hadn't enjoyed practice, and even though she'd done well in the games, she hadn't had a very good time. Over the summer she had decided that she wouldn't play this year because it made her uncomfortable to be around her former friends. It had been a difficult decision, but one she thought she had to make. Even though she'd signed up for gym, which basically meant she was intending to play on a sports team, she still hadn't made her final decision.

But now everything had changed. Now they were all getting along again. She could go to practice and feel like she used to when the three of them worked as a team. She'd missed that, and she was glad to have the opportunity to get it back.

"Oh, yeah," Kate said, feeling happier than she had in a long time. "I am *so* there."

"Jess and I are going to train in the fall intramural league. You *have* to come, too. That way we'll be ready when the season starts for real," Tara said eagerly.

"I'm just bummed that most of the games are going to be on Tuesdays," said Jessica, putting the lid on her container and starting to peel a banana. "I was going to work Tuesdays at the restaurant. It's bowling league night, and you'd be amazed how well those guys tip. But I'm giving it all up to be with you guys."

"You're such a giver," Tara said with mock sincerity.

"Tuesdays?" Kate said, a horrible feeling beginning to grow inside of her.

Jessica nodded. "I checked out the schedule on the coach's door this morning."

"You don't sound happy about that," said Tara. "Is there something wrong with Tuesdays?"

Kate wasn't sure what to say. Tuesday night was the night her Wicca study group met. There was no way she was going to stop going to that. But she really wanted to be able to start her basketball season early. Giving that up now that she was looking forward to it again was going to be really tough, but not as tough as explaining to Tara and Jessica *why* she was giving it up.

"I don't know if I can make Tuesdays," she said carefully. "I'm already committed to something else on that night."

"What could be more important than basketball?" Tara asked. "You've never missed a game. Remember that time you had the flu and still played? You made seventeen points and then threw up in the locker room. The coach was furious at you for not telling her you were sick."

"Yeah," said Kate, remembering the game well. "But we won, didn't we?"

"Exactly my point," Tara replied. "So what's this other gig you've got going?"

"Nothing exciting,"Kate answered, trying to sound casual. "Just something I said I'd do. I'll see if I can get out of it."

"You'd better," said Jessica. "Now that Linda Thomson has graduated you have a good chance of starting in games, and this fall season will give you even more of an edge. None of the juniors from last year are nearly as quick as you are. We need you, Morgan. Don't let us down."

Jessica said the last part of her statement in an imitation of Coach Saliers, their junior varsity coach. It sounded so much like her, and like something that she would say, that Kate and Tara howled with laughter. As they laughed, Kate glanced over and saw Sherrie glaring at them. She was tempted to give her a little wave, but she resisted the urge. Sherrie was beaten. There was no sense in rubbing it in. Kate had what she wanted, and she was content to let Sherrie lick her wounds.

But that didn't solve her problem of what to do about the team. How was she going to be in two places at one time? It just wasn't possible. She couldn't think about that now, though. It could wait. She was having too much fun being with Jessica and Tara to let that ruin things.

"I have to ask you something," Jessica said after they'd calmed down a little. "It's about your buddy Cooper."

"Cooper?" said Kate. "What about her?"

"Well, I heard something about her," Jessica said.

"Oh, no, she's into guys," said Kate before Jessica could finish. "A lot of people think she isn't, though, because she's kind of a loner and all."

"It's not that," Jessica said, rolling her eyes. "But thanks for the clarification. No, it's something else." She paused.

"What?" Kate asked, wondering what Jessica might have heard.

"One of the waitresses at the restaurant heard her perform at Big Mouth a few weeks ago," Jessica said. "She said Cooper did this really great piece. I guess it really blew people away. It was about witches and being burned at the stake or something like that."

"And?" Kate asked while thinking. *Thank God Annie didn't use her real name when she performed or Jess would be asking about her, too.*

"Now she's wearing some kind of occult symbol," Jessica continued. "You know, that star thing. What's with that?"

Kate shrugged. "I didn't go to the Big Mouth performance," she said. "And I didn't notice the necklace."

She hoped she sounded convincing. Why did

Jessica have to bring this up now? Cooper didn't think anyone would notice her pentacle, but Annie had told Kate that her boyfriend Brian had said something about it the day before, and now Jessica was asking questions. *I knew something like this would happen*, Kate thought grimly.

"Some people are saying she's into black magic," said Tara.

Kate looked up. "What do you mean?" she said sharply. "Cooper would never do anything like that."

Tara shrugged. "I'm just telling you what I heard. Some of the girls in my English class said they saw her coming out of that occult store downtown."

"Crones' Circle?" Kate asked, already knowing the answer to her question. "So what? It's just a bookstore."

"I hear they do weird rituals there," said Jessica. "Cindy Miller bought some kind of candle there that was supposed to bring her good luck, and she said they offered to do a spell for her if she paid them."

"They wouldn't do that!" Kate said angrily. "They would never do a spell for someone for money!"

She knew that either Jessica had her story wrong or that Cindy had lied. No self-respecting witch would do a spell for money, and certainly no one at Crones' Circle would ever suggest that.

Jessica looked taken aback. "Relax," she said. "It's

not like the people at the store are friends of yours or anything. I'm just passing along information."

What Kate wanted to say was, "But they *are* friends of mine." She wanted to tell Tara and Jessica that Sophia, Archer, and the others who owned and ran Crones' Circle were good people. She wanted to tell them that she knew they were good because every week she went there to learn about witchcraft. If she could just tell them that then she could explain to them why Cooper was wearing a pentacle and what it meant.

Instead she said, "I'm sorry. It's just that Cooper gets a bad rap. She's really nice, but people have all these weird ideas about what she does and what she's like."

"Well, it doesn't help that she wears that thing and doesn't talk to anybody except you and Annie," said Jessica.

"You just have to get to know her." Kate said weakly. But *would* Jessica and Tara ever really get to know Cooper and Annie? Tara had already spent a little bit of time with them, but she didn't really know them well. And Jessica had never said more than a few words to either of them. What would happen if they suddenly all started hanging out together? Would all of them get along? Suddenly her renewed friendship with Tara and Jessica didn't seem as perfect a situation as it had half an hour before.

"Well, I've got to get going," Jessica said, putting

her trash into her lunch bag and crinkling it up. "I've got homework already and I need to hit the library for a few minutes."

"I'll go with you," Tara told her. "I'm going to stop by the gym and pick up a copy of the intramural schedule. Kate? You coming?"

Kate shook her head. "You guys go ahead," she said.

"Okay," said Tara. "Do you want me to pick you up a copy of the schedule, too?"

"Sure," said Kate. "Thanks." *I don't know if I'll use it or not, though,* she thought sadly.

"Hey," Jessica said as she and Tara stood up to leave. "How about a movie this weekend? Maybe Annie and Cooper would like to come, too."

"That would be fun," Kate answered. "I'll ask them and give you a call tonight, okay?"

"You're on," Jessica answered.

She and Tara left, leaving Kate alone at the table with her thoughts. What was she going to do? She'd thought that working things out with Tyler was her biggest problem. Now she had a whole pile of problems. Worst of all, it was because something good had happened. Her former best friends were back in her life. Not only that, but they seemed interested in getting to know her newer friends. She should feel happy about that. But her excitement was dampened by the fact that now there was even more pressure for her to figure out how to integrate the two lives she'd been living for the past six months—

the one involving Wicca and the one most people thought she was leading.

She looked over at Sherrie. She was still sitting alone. As Kate looked at her former friend she couldn't help thinking, *Maybe this is worse than anything Sherrie could have dreamed up for me herself.*

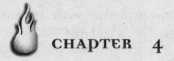

CHAPTER 4

"I can't believe we're about to see a movie with the Graces," Cooper said as she stood with Kate, Sasha, and Annie outside the theater. "Isn't that one of the signs of the end of the world?"

"It's going to be fine," Kate told her. "Jessica and Tara are great. It was Sherrie who was the problem." She glanced at Cooper's neck.

"Don't worry," Cooper said, seeing her look. "I tucked it under my shirt."

It was Saturday afternoon. The four of them had just finished having lunch, over which Kate had asked Cooper to keep her pentacle out of sight. She'd waited until just before they were supposed to meet Tara and Jessica because she knew that would give Cooper less time to throw a fit about it. It had been difficult enough convincing her to go to the movie in the first place.

"I can't believe your friends think I worship the devil," Cooper said, leaning against the wall.

"They don't think you worship the devil," said

Kate. "They just think you're weird."

"Oh, that's lots better," replied Cooper.

"I'm not the one who told you to wear that thing," Kate told her. "But I did tell you it would cause trouble."

"So a few people saw it and asked some questions," said Cooper. "Big deal. You got out of it, right?"

"Yeah, by lying," answered Kate.

"And if *you* weren't still in the broom closet, you wouldn't have to lie," Cooper said triumphantly.

Kate shot her a look. They had been through this discussion dozens of times, and she knew that they weren't going to get anywhere going through it again, especially since Jessica and Tara were walking up the street toward them.

"Be nice," Kate ordered Cooper, who smiled sweetly.

"Hey," Jessica said as she and Tara reached the others.

"Hi," Kate said. "You guys know everybody, right?"

Tara and Jessica nodded. "Hey, guys," they said.

"So what are we seeing?" Tara asked, looking at the different movies playing at the theater.

"I cast my vote for Mel Gibson," Sasha said instantly. "Very yummy."

Annie and Jessica groaned in unison. "No way," Annie said. "How about the Julia Roberts comedy?"

"Or the new Shakespeare with Kenneth Branagh?" suggested Jessica.

"Too arty," declared Tara. "I'm all over that slasher film they've been advertising to death. You know, the one with that girl from the Bioré commercials."

"You're all nuts," said Cooper decidedly. "How can you pass up a chance to see the director's cut of *Close Encounters of the Third Kind*? It hasn't been re-released since before we were all born."

"Not again," Annie wailed. "Kate, there's one vote for each film. You're the deciding vote."

Kate looked at the marquee. Then she looked around at her friends. They were all looking at her beseechingly. She knew each of them wanted her to pick the film she wanted to see. But what did *Kate* want to see? She went over the choices in her mind.

"Well?" Cooper asked after a minute had gone by. "Will it be dumbbell Mel, airhead Julia, a lot of British people in costumes, a bunch of dead teenagers, or the most brilliant science fiction film of all time?"

Kate thought some more, chewing on her lip while she looked at the posters for the movies that lined the walls of the theater entrance. Then she looked at her friends.

"Give me your money," she ordered. "I'll get the tickets and surprise you."

Grudgingly, they all reached into their pockets and handed her their cash. Kate counted it carefully before smiling and saying, "I'll be right back."

She walked to the box office and returned a minute later with six tickets in her hand. "Here you go," she said as she handed them around.

"What's this?" exclaimed Cooper as she read her ticket. "None of us picked this one."

"I did," Kate said firmly. "You said I was the deciding vote, and this is what I voted for. I think it looks good."

The five other girls looked at each other and then looked at Kate. "You're sneaky," Jessica said.

"Next time I get to be the deciding vote," Sasha added. "And we're seeing Mel."

"Come on," Kate said, heading for the doors. "It starts in ten minutes."

Two hours later they walked out again.

"I told you it would be good," Kate said triumphantly. "And wasn't it?"

"It was okay," Cooper admitted.

"It was more than okay," insisted Kate. "Where have you ever seen special effects like that before? And George Clooney has never looked better."

"All right already," said Jessica. "So you picked an okay film. It's not like you solved the Mideast peace problem."

"It wasn't far from it," commented Kate. "Getting all five of you to agree on something requires about as much negotiating skill."

"Hey," said Annie. "I think we did pretty well for our first time out together."

"Me, too," agreed Tara.

"So what's next?" Sasha asked. "Anyone for sodas?"

They stopped, trying to decide where to go next. Before they could come to a decision someone walked up to them. "Hey there," said a voice.

Kate turned and saw Archer standing behind her. She was carrying some shopping bags and was wearing a T-shirt that said BLESSED BE on it.

"Oh, hi," Kate said, glancing at Archer's shirt nervously.

Annie, Cooper, and Sasha all greeted Archer warmly. Jessica and Tara looked at her and smiled.

"These are my friends Tara and Jess," Kate said, introducing them to Archer.

She smiled. "Nice to meet you. I was just out running some errands, but now I've got to get back to the store. I'll see you guys on Tuesday, though, right?"

"We'll be there," Annie told her.

Archer left and Jessica turned to Kate. "That's one of the women from that store we were talking about yesterday, right?"

"Um, yeah," said Kate, suddenly wishing that Archer hadn't happened by when she did.

"Is that what you have to do on Tuesdays?" asked Tara. "Something at her store?"

Kate looked helplessly at Annie and Cooper. What was she supposed to say? She hadn't thought of a story to tell Tara and Jessica yet, as she hadn't planned on the topic's coming up so soon. The silence seemed to stretch out forever as she stood there trying to think of what to say next.

"Yeah, we go there every Tuesday night," Cooper said finally. "Me, Annie, and Kate."

Kate looked at her in horror. Was Cooper about to tell their secret? How could she? She knew that Jessica and Tara didn't know about their involvement in Wicca. What was Cooper thinking?

"We go there for a reading group," Cooper continued. "You know, a book group. Like Oprah's. Only this one is all about fantasy and science fiction books. You know, Tolkien, Marion Zimmer Bradley, Frank Herbert. That kind of stuff."

Jessica nodded. "I get it," she said. "That's how you knew all about the store," she added to Kate. "Why didn't you just tell us you were in a reading group? What's the big deal about that?"

"I guess I just thought you might think it was sort of weird," Kate said, relieved that Cooper had come up with a believable story. "You know, science fiction and fantasy are kind of geeky."

"I happen to love them," Jessica said. "Maybe I'll come along one of these nights."

"Oh, you can't," Annie said quickly.

Jessica looked puzzled.

"I mean, the group is closed to new members right now," Annie added hastily. "It was getting too big, so we decided to limit it to twenty. But if someone drops out you can come."

"Right," said Kate. "Then we'd be glad to have you."

Jessica nodded. "Okay," she said. "But Kate,

what about Tuesday night games?"

"Games?" Cooper and Annie said.

Out of the frying pan and into the fire, Kate thought. Just when she'd thought she was out of the woods, Jessica had to go and bring up basketball. Kate hadn't yet told Annie and Cooper about the intramural league games scheduled on the same nights as class.

"There's a fall intramural league we're in, and the games are mostly on Tuesday nights this year," Tara said, doing Kate's work for her. "I guess you'll just have to skip the group on those nights, Kate."

"Kate, will you be skipping class?" Cooper asked her friend, raising one eyebrow teasingly.

"I'm trying to work all of that out," Kate answered carefully.

Cooper made a noncommittal noise, and Annie gave Kate a look that indicated her displeasure, but neither of them said anything.

"How about those sodas?" Kate suggested. "I'm really thirsty all of a sudden."

Later that evening, after saying good-bye to Tara and Jessica, Kate, Cooper, Annie, and Sasha were sitting in Annie's bedroom. Now that they were away from the other girls, Kate's friends were letting her know in no uncertain terms just how they felt about what had happened.

"I can't believe I had to tell them that we go to a *book* group!" Cooper said. She was pacing the room like a tiger in a cage, and Kate knew she was angry. She couldn't blame her. She didn't feel very good about what had happened either. At the same time, she had to admit that she was relieved that her secret was still safe from Jessica and Tara.

"I couldn't just spring it on them right there," she said in her own defense. "I mean, it wasn't like I knew Archer was going to show up and mention class."

"You could have told them yesterday," Cooper argued. "You know, when you were all busy trying to pretend you didn't know what my pentacle was."

"That's not fair," said Kate. "I defended you."

"I don't need defending," Cooper said. "That's the whole point, Kate. I'm not ashamed of having Wicca as part of my life. Neither is Annie. You're the only one who keeps hiding it. And when you hide it then we end up having to hide it, too. It isn't fair. Tyler already told you that he can't live like that. Well, neither can we."

"What are you saying?" Kate asked, afraid to hear the answer.

"I'm saying that I won't lie anymore," Cooper told her. "If Jessica and Tara ask me what my pentacle is, or what we really do at the store, I'm going to tell them."

Kate was quiet for a moment. "Is that how you feel, too?" she asked Annie.

Annie sighed. "You really *do* make it hard sometimes," she said. "I didn't mind so much when it was just your parents, but now that we're going to be hanging around with Jessica and Tara, I think you have to make some serious choices."

"Like what you're going to do about the basketball league," Cooper said.

"That's not your problem," Kate snapped, sounding angrier than she wanted to.

"Yeah, it is," Cooper answered just as angrily. "We're all in this together, remember?"

"Then why am I the only one who feels trapped by it?" Kate asked, near tears. "Why am I the only one who has to deal with this stuff? I thought this year was going to be fun. But you guys all get to have lunch together while I watch Sherrie chew her stupid carrot sticks. Annie gets to be the assistant editor of the paper. You get to do your music and creative writing. Sasha gets to be in drama club. I don't even get to play basketball. Oh, and my boyfriend has pretty much dumped me. Let's not forget that. Why is it all happening to me?"

Her friends looked at her for a moment as she fought back tears. Then Annie spoke. "You're not the only one things are happening to," she said softly. "We've all had our share of challenges. You know that."

"I know," Kate said, wiping her eyes. "But it feels like that right now. All kinds of good things are happening for you guys and I just keep having problem after problem dumped on me."

"Actually, it's just one big problem in different forms," Cooper told her.

"That doesn't make it any easier," replied Kate. "And it doesn't help me figure out how to solve it."

"I think you know how," said Cooper.

"I know what you think I should do," Kate replied. "But I don't appreciate being forced to do it just because you want to wear that necklace."

"Hey," Cooper said. "I told you I wouldn't hide who I am for anyone. I'm wearing this because it's important to me. If other people have a problem with it, let them talk to me about it. You could have told Jessica and Tara to ask me for themselves."

"But then you would have told them!" said Kate.

Cooper nodded. "That's right," she said. "And they would have learned something."

"Did you tell Annie's boyfriend what it means?" she asked.

Cooper looked down. "No," she admitted. "I told him it was a good luck charm."

"Then why can't I just tell people the same thing?" Kate asked. "Why doesn't Annie have to tell Brian about what she's doing but I have to tell everyone?"

"I haven't told Brian yet because I haven't known him very long," Annie said. "I want him to know me better first. But you've known your friends since you were like infants or something. They already know you as a person. The same with your parents."

"I don't think that will make it any easier," said Kate.

Sasha hadn't said a word throughout the entire discussion. Now she cleared her throat and spoke. "Kate, do you remember when you first confronted me about being a runaway?" she asked.

"How could I forget?" answered Kate. "You ran out of that diner so fast I thought you were in the Olympic trials."

Sasha smiled. "I ran away because I was embarrassed," she said. "I didn't know what you would think of me, and I was afraid that you would reject me."

"But I didn't," Kate said.

"Right," said Sasha. "But I had to give you that chance, didn't I? If I had just gone on hiding it from you, you might never have found out. Then I would probably have skipped town when things got too hard, and I'd still be running."

"What are you saying?" Kate asked her.

"I'm saying that sometimes you have to give other people a chance," said Sasha. "Jessica and Tara might be more understanding than you think."

"Maybe," Kate admitted. "But I know my parents won't be. I just know it."

"So start small," said Annie. "Tell Jessica and Tara. You don't have to make a big deal out of it or anything. Just tell them you're taking the class. They don't have to know everything."

"But they just started speaking to me again," Kate protested. "What if they cut me off like before?"

"Then you won't be any worse off than you were then," Cooper told her. "Would you rather have them not knowing the real you?"

"Yes," said Kate frankly. "And that still doesn't solve the problem of class being on the same night as some of our games," she added.

"Can't help you there," Annie said. "But let's take things one step at a time."

"You sound like this is a group project," Kate said. "I'm the one who has to take the steps."

"Yes," said Annie, sitting on the bed and putting her arm around her friend. "But we'll be right behind you."

"Gee, thanks," Kate said, leaning her head on Annie's shoulder. "Can I come live with you when my parents throw me out of the house?"

"Sure," said Annie. "But you'll have to bunk with Meg. I'm not sharing my room."

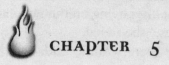

CHAPTER 5

Cooper looked at the slip of paper in her hand. Ms. Carter had handed it to her a few minutes earlier, when Cooper had arrived at her creative writing class. It was a request from the principal, Mrs. Browning, for Cooper to come see her. As Cooper walked to the main office she tried to imagine what the principal wanted. Had something terrible happened to one of her parents? She prayed that wasn't the case. But why else would Mrs. Browning call her out of class in the middle of the day to talk to her?

She pushed open the office door and went in. Mrs. Browning's assistant, a tall nervous man named Ethan Mathers, was sitting behind his desk shuffling some papers around noisily. When he saw Cooper standing in front of him he smiled weakly. Cooper handed him the slip, and he looked at it carefully.

"Just one minute," he said. "I'll let her know you're here." He picked up his phone, punched a button, and a moment later said into the receiver, "Cooper Rivers is here." When he hung up he nodded toward the closed door of the principal's office. "Go on in."

Cooper went to the door and turned the knob, pushing the door open slowly. She looked inside and saw Mrs. Browning seated behind a large mahogany desk. She was looking at something on a computer screen. When she saw Cooper she smiled. "Come in," she said cheerfully. "I'll be right with you."

Cooper stepped into the room and shut the door behind her. The tone of the principal's voice made her feel less nervous. *If it was bad news, she wouldn't have sounded so cheerful*, she thought as she sat down in one of the two chairs positioned in front of the desk.

Principal Browning clicked away at her keyboard for a moment more and then turned to look at Cooper. "Budgets," she said, sounding weary. "Every year everybody wants more money and there's less to go around. If this keeps up we'll be having bake sales every day."

Cooper smiled. She'd always liked Mrs. Browning, who in spite of her position always seemed to maintain a sense of humor.

"I guess you're wondering why I called you in here," the principal said.

Cooper nodded. "I thought someone had died," she said.

Mrs. Browning laughed. "No," she said. "At least not yet. But we still have two more periods to go."

"So what is it, then?" asked Cooper.

The principal sighed. "Mrs. Greeley came to see me today," she said.

"Mrs. Greeley?" Cooper repeated. "About what?"

"About you," Principal Browning replied.

"Me?" said Cooper, confused. "What about me? What did I do, I mean besides try to stay awake in her class?"

Almost immediately she realized that what she'd said wasn't very polite. She started to apologize but then saw that Mrs. Browning was suppressing a smile.

"I know Hazel's style can be a little daunting," the principal said diplomatically. "But no, that's not why she came to see me. She's concerned about you."

Cooper shook her head. "I still don't get it," she said. "I go to class. I don't nap during her lectures. What's to worry about?"

The principal leaned back in her chair. "Actually, it's that necklace you're wearing," she said.

"My necklace?" exclaimed Cooper. "What about it?" She was now even more confused than when she'd first gotten the summons to Mrs. Browning's office.

Principal Browning looked at the pentacle that Cooper had instinctively reached up to touch. "Do you know what that is?" she asked.

Cooper nodded. "Of course I do," she said.

The principal folded her hands on her desk. "Over the summer a number of the teachers took a class," she said slowly. "It was a program designed to help educators identify students who might be—" She paused, as if searching for the right word.

"Might be what?" Cooper asked warily.

"Who might be having personal problems or who might be potential threats to the other students," Mrs. Browning said, sighing.

"But—" Cooper said, immediately jumping to her own defense.

The principal held up her hand. "I know," she said. "I don't think you're any kind of threat to anyone. You're one of the brightest and most creative students here."

Cooper looked at her, confused. Principal Browning had always been kind to her, but she'd never said such nice things before. Why was she saying them now?

The principal looked at Cooper. "I don't have to tell you that high schools in this country aren't always the safest places to be," she said.

"Sure," Cooper said, shrugging her shoulders. "But I still don't get what any of this has to do with me and my necklace."

"One of the things that a lot of troubled teenagers have in common is an interest in Satanism and the occult," Mrs. Browning told her.

Cooper snorted. "Now I get it," she said. "Mrs. Greeley thinks I'm going to come in and waste the entire class because of my necklace."

"One of the signs we learned about in the

course we took was the pentagram," the principal said. "When Mrs. Greeley saw you wearing one she became concerned."

"That's because she has no idea what it really is!" Cooper protested. "It's not Satanic! It's perfectly harmless!"

"Maybe so," Mrs. Browning said calmly. "But the fact is that people associate it with things that aren't harmless."

"That's because they're ignorant," said Cooper angrily.

The principal looked at her darkly. "You know better than that," she said. "Just because *you* understand what it means doesn't mean everyone else does. And you know that there are people who associate that symbol with things that are potentially dangerous."

"But I don't," Cooper said. "You know I'm not going to come in here and shoot the place up, so everyone can just stop worrying about me."

"It's not you we're worried about," explained Principal Browning. "It's the other students. We don't want them to feel uncomfortable."

"Oh, no, we wouldn't want to do that," Cooper replied sarcastically. "Goddess forbid they have to learn something or expand their horizons."

"That's not helping," the principal said.

"Sorry," Cooper said. "But I don't see why I have to be singled out because other people have ridiculous ideas about what a pentagram means."

"I understand that," Mrs. Browning replied. "I really do. But I also have to worry about the other six hundred and forty-two students in this school. If they feel threatened then they come to me, and I have to deal with it."

"Does anyone feel threatened by my necklace?" asked Cooper.

"Actually, yes," the principal answered.

"Who?" asked Cooper, genuinely surprised.

"You know I can't tell you that," Mrs. Browning said. "But several people in addition to Mrs. Greeley have come to see me about this."

Cooper didn't say anything for a minute. She sat in her chair, looking at Principal Browning and wondering who else might have complained about her necklace. Whoever they were, she wished she could find them and give them a piece of her mind.

"I want you to do me a favor," the principal said.

"Which is?" Cooper asked sullenly.

"Stop wearing that pentagram," she said.

"It's called a pentacle," Cooper said. "A pentagram is when you draw it on something. A pentacle is when it's in physical form."

Mrs. Browning smiled slightly. "Thanks for clearing that up," she said. "Will you stop wearing the pentacle?"

Cooper stared at her, not knowing what to say. Her mind was racing with all kinds of thoughts and feelings. She liked Mrs. Browning, but the principal was asking her to do something she didn't want to do. She couldn't see any reason why she should stop wearing the pentacle. It wasn't hurting anyone. Just because a few people didn't understand what it meant shouldn't mean that she shouldn't be allowed to wear it. That was like giving in, something she hated doing.

"I'll think about it," she said finally.

Mrs. Browning took a deep breath. "Okay," she said. "But don't think too long. I'd appreciate it if you didn't show up tomorrow wearing it."

"Like I said, I'll think about it," Cooper repeated. "Can I go now?"

The principal nodded and Cooper stood up. As Cooper reached for the door, Principal Browning said, "Cooper."

Cooper turned and waited for the principal to speak.

"Compromising isn't the same as abandoning your principles," Mrs. Browning said.

Cooper gave a little laugh, but it wasn't a happy one. "That's funny," she said. "I said almost the same thing to my boyfriend a couple of weeks ago."

"Then you understand what I'm saying," Mrs. Browning replied.

"I understand it," answered Cooper. "I'm just not sure I believe it this time."

She left the office and walked into the hallway. She was angry, and she wasn't sure where she was going. She didn't want to go back to class. She was too upset to concentrate on writing anything.

Besides, there were only fifteen minutes left in the period anyway. There was no point in going back.

She stormed through the hallways, trying to think of who might have gone to Mrs. Browning about her. She wasn't surprised that Mrs. Greeley would do such a thing, but other students? Who would possibly think that she was a potential threat? And who would go to the trouble of actually reporting her to the principal?

Sherrie, she thought suddenly. Sherrie would do something like that. But she was only one person. Mrs. Browning had said that several people had come to see her. Maybe Sherrie was one of them. The more Cooper thought about it the more sure she was of that. But who else? Now that Jessica and Tara weren't following her every order, Sherrie didn't have that many friends. *But I bet the ones she does have would believe her if she told them a lot of lies about me*, Cooper thought angrily.

The bell for the next period rang. Where was she supposed to be? English. In Mr. Tharpe's room. She really didn't want to go, but Annie was in that class, and if anyone would help her calm down it was Annie.

Cooper walked to the classroom and went inside. She was relieved to see that Annie was already there, looking at the book they were going to begin discussing in class.

"You won't believe what just happened," Cooper said as she sat down beside her friend.

"Principal Browning just asked me to stop wearing my pentacle. Apparently, Greeley and a couple of kids complained about it."

Annie looked at her, stunned. "Can they do that?" she asked.

"Apparently," Cooper replied. "They're afraid that people will get the wrong idea about me and be afraid."

"Aren't most of them already afraid of you?" asked Annie, earning a glare from Cooper.

"Mrs. Browning said that my pentacle makes some people feel unsafe coming to school."

Annie let out a long sigh. "What are you going to do?"

"I was hoping you would have some ideas," Cooper told her. "You're the practical one, right? I'm the one who yells and stamps her feet. I don't think that's going to work this time."

Annie looked thoughtful. "Maybe there *is* something I can do," she said. "But not before tomorrow."

"What is it?" Cooper asked.

Annie shook her head. "I don't want to say anything in case it doesn't work out," she said. "The big issue right now is whether or not you're going to wear the necklace tomorrow."

Cooper shrugged. "I haven't decided yet," she answered. "I have to think about it."

She *did* think about it, all during Mr. Tharpe's class. She tried to pay attention to what he was saying about the novel they were reading, but her mind kept wandering back to her discussion with Principal Browning. She hadn't exactly ordered Cooper not to wear the pentacle. She had simply asked her not to. What was she going to do if Cooper *did* wear it?

Cooper was torn. It would have been one thing if Mrs. Browning had been unpleasant about the situation. But she was a nice woman, and she had treated Cooper like an adult. Cooper didn't agree with the principal's reasons for asking her to not wear the pentacle, but she understood Mrs. Browning's points. Sort of.

Compromise. She had to laugh when she thought about the principal's asking her to compromise. It was the same thing she'd asked of T.J. a few weeks before when they'd had a disagreement. Ironically, their fight had been over Cooper's involvement in Wicca, too. T.J. didn't want her to be so public about her interest in it because he was afraid it would cause trouble for her. Now she *was* in trouble for being visible. But it wasn't the kind of trouble that T.J. was worried about. He was afraid that people would try to hurt her. This was almost worse. She couldn't even fight her accusers in this case because she didn't know who they were.

Why couldn't people understand that her wearing a pentacle was a sign of how proud she was to be studying witchcraft? Why did it have to mean something sinister? Just because a bunch of stupid people who wanted to think they were into something weird misused the sign of the pentagram was no reason why she should have to give it up. It wasn't her fault that heavy metal bands scrawled pentagrams on their album covers and people who didn't know any better drew them on stuff to try to scare people or to try to look cool.

She realized that she was playing with her necklace, holding it in her hand and pulling on it as she thought. Had she done that before? Is that why people had noticed it? It wasn't like she flashed it around or anything. People would have to look pretty hard to even see what she was wearing. Usually, it was tucked under the collar of whatever shirt she was wearing.

She tucked it inside, hiding it from view. She didn't want to give anyone any reason to complain that she was showing it off or anything. Now she could feel it against her skin, the metal warm from being in her hand. Was it really such a big deal to her to be able to wear it? She asked herself this, as well as other questions, as she waited for class to end. Why was she wearing the pentacle? True, it had been part of the ritual she'd done with her friends. That was one reason. But would she have worn it if it didn't have that meaning to her?

What did wearing the necklace really mean to her? Was she wearing it to shock people? She had to admit that part of her liked the idea that people would see it and wonder why she had it on. But was that a good enough reason to insist on keeping it on? Or was there another reason, one that went deeper than just making a statement?

She looked down and discovered that she had been drawing pentagrams in her notebook. The page was filled with five-pointed stars. Cooper looked at them. In a child's drawing they would have just been stars. But they meant much more than that. To her they represented one of the fundamental principles of Wicca—the fact that everything in life is connected. Each of the lines joining the arms to one another was like an electrical wire. Energy flowed through them, allowing the powers of the elements represented by the five points to combine.

Earth. Air. Fire. Water. She named each arm as she drew another pentagram. And then the fifth point, representing Spirit, the unseen element uniting all things. She drew the final line and looked at the design. It was so simple and so perfect. How could anyone see anything malicious in it? To her it was absolutely beautiful—five paths joined into one. It was a symbol both of what she believed and of what she was trying to do with her life, unite the different energies within and around her to create something powerful and magical.

Yes, she decided, it was important to her to be able to wear her pentacle. It wasn't just something she was doing to stand out. It was something she wore to remind herself of what she was studying and what she hoped to accomplish by her involvement in the Craft. She wasn't ashamed of it, and she wasn't going to hide it.

Reaching into her shirt, she pulled the pentacle out again. She let it hang freely for anyone to see. *And if they don't like it*, she thought, *they can tell me to my face*.

CHAPTER 6

The next morning Cooper, Annie, and Kate met Sasha a few blocks from school and walked the rest of the way together. Cooper had filled her friends in on the events of the day before, and they all knew what had happened in Mrs. Browning's office. She'd also told them about her decision to keep wearing the pentacle.

"Are you sure you want to do this?" Kate asked as they neared the entrance to the building. "We won't think any less of you if you decide not to wear it."

"Thanks," Cooper replied. "But I would think less of myself if I didn't."

Of all her friends, Kate was being the least supportive, which didn't surprise Cooper. She knew that Kate worried more about what other people thought than she, Annie, or Sasha did. In fact, Kate had been the only one to actively try to persuade her to go along with Principal Browning. But ultimately her reasons for wanting Cooper to give in hadn't swayed her, and Cooper had decided to go ahead with her original plan.

"Who knows," said Sasha. "Maybe nothing will happen. Maybe those people who complained will just back off."

"We're about to find out," said Cooper as they walked up the school steps.

They pushed open the doors and walked down the hall to the lockers. Cooper noticed a couple of people looking at her as she walked by, and she wondered if somehow word had gotten out about Mrs. Browning's request. Certainly people couldn't be looking at her for any other reason. She'd gone out of her way to dress—with the exception of the pentacle—more conservatively than usual. She was wearing jeans and a plain denim shirt over a white T-shirt. The pentacle was visible above the collar of the T-shirt, but there was nothing to draw attention to it.

"So far, so good," Annie remarked as they reached their lockers.

"Not so fast," Kate remarked. "Principal at three o'clock."

Cooper looked to her right and saw Principal Browning walking toward them, a neutral expression on her face.

How could she have heard so quickly? Cooper wondered. *Someone must have run and told her the minute I walked in.*

Mrs. Browning stopped in front of Cooper. "I

see you decided not to take it off," she said.

"That's right," said Cooper. "This symbol is important to me, and I don't see why I should have to remove it just because some people don't understand it."

The principal sighed. "Let's talk about this in my office," she said quietly.

Cooper looked around and saw that a small crowd had formed. "No," she said. "We can talk here."

"Cooper," Mrs. Browning said. "Don't make this difficult."

"I'm not the one making it difficult," Cooper said loudly enough for those around her to hear. "It's someone else in this school, someone who's afraid to talk to me directly. Anything you have to say to me you can say here. That way everyone will know what's going on."

The principal looked unhappy. "Fine," she said. "I'm going to ask you once more. Will you please take off that necklace?"

Cooper looked around at the assembled students. She noticed Sherrie standing toward the back, watching everything intently. Once again Cooper wondered if the other girl was behind the principal's request. But it didn't really matter. It had become a larger issue now.

"No," she said firmly. "I'm not taking it off."

Principal Browning looked around. "Then I'm afraid I'm going to have to suspend you," she said.

"Suspend her?" Sasha said indignantly. "For wearing a necklace?"

"A necklace that is offensive and threatening to other students," the principal replied. "And yes, I'm suspending her. You'll have to leave school immediately. When you're ready to discuss this situation we can talk about the conditions of your return. I'll call your parents."

Mrs. Browning looked into Cooper's eyes. Cooper held her gaze, refusing to back down. Finally the principal looked away. "I'm sorry," she said so that only Cooper could hear. "You left me with no choice."

"I guess that makes both of us," Cooper answered. She grabbed her backpack from her still-open locker, slammed the door, and turned around.

Sasha, Kate, and Annie followed her as she walked back to the front doors.

"What are you going to do?" Kate asked anxiously.

"I have no idea," said Cooper. "Watch a lot of television, I guess."

"I'm serious, Cooper," Kate said. "You can't just not come back, and they won't let you back until you agree not to wear the pentacle."

"Then we'll just have to see who blinks first," Cooper told her. She paused at the door and looked at her friends. "Thanks for walking with me," she said. "I'll see you tonight at class."

She left the building and walked quickly down

the steps. The others watched her as she turned left at the end of the walk and started toward home.

"She is so stubborn sometimes," Kate said, sounding frustrated.

"That's our Cooper," agreed Annie.

"Do you really think she'll stick it out?" Sasha asked them.

Kate and Annie looked at each other.

"Knowing Cooper—yeah, she will," Annie said.

A moment later a noticeably upset T.J. came running up to them. "What happened to Cooper?" he asked anxiously. "Everyone is saying she just got thrown out of school."

"That didn't take long," Sasha remarked.

"She wasn't exactly thrown out," Annie said, trying to calm T.J. down. "Principal Browning asked her to leave."

T.J. held up his hands, looking very confused. "Why would she do that?" he asked.

Annie looked at Kate and Sasha for help. She knew that Cooper hadn't mentioned the issue to T.J. She hadn't wanted to upset him, and she hadn't thought things would go so far so quickly.

"She refused to stop wearing her pentacle necklace," Kate said.

T.J. slammed his hand against the wall. "I *knew* something like this would happen," he said, almost shouting. "I told her she was going to get into hot water if she insisted on talking about this stuff."

"She wasn't talking about it," said Annie. "She was just wearing a necklace."

"It's the same thing," said T.J. argumentatively.

Annie was surprised at how upset he was. Normally, T.J. was a soft-spoken guy who rarely raised his voice. But now he was really angry, pacing around and hitting the wall as he talked.

"Why doesn't she ever listen?" he said. "Why does she always have to be right?"

Annie put her hand on his arm. "It's really not that big a deal," she said.

"Yeah," T.J. said, shaking her hand off. "It *is* that big a deal. I'll see you guys later."

"T.J.!" Annie called after his retreating form, but he kept walking.

"Great," she said. "That was very helpful."

"You can't blame him," said Kate. "One of his big fears just came true."

Annie looked at her. She knew Kate was right. But that didn't help.

"Hey, is it true that your friend is into some weird cult?"

A girl had come up to Sasha, Kate, and Annie. She was a freshman, and none of them had ever seen her before. She was with two friends who hung back, watching her but not saying anything.

"No," Annie said. "She's not in a cult. Where did you hear that?"

The girl blushed. "Some kids were talking about it just a minute ago," she said. "They said she was into Satanism or something."

"Well, she's not," Kate snapped. "You shouldn't believe everything you hear."

Kate turned and walked away from the girl and from her friends. Annie and Sasha ran after her.

"Hey," Annie said. "She was just asking a question. A lot of people are going to want to know what happened. We might as well get used to it."

"I know," Kate said. "But I can't help but think that T.J. was right. We warned Cooper about this."

"Saying I told you so isn't going to help," replied Annie.

As they neared the end of the hallway Jessica and Tara rounded it, almost running into them. Seeing them, Kate looked at Annie and made a face.

"There you guys are," Tara said. "We've been looking all over for you. What's up with Cooper?"

"What have you heard?" Kate asked.

"That she went off on Browning and got kicked out for a week," Jessica answered.

"I can't believe this," Kate said. "Not ten minutes has gone by and already people have managed to make up a dozen different stories."

"What really happened?" asked Jessica.

"Cooper refused to take off the necklace she wears," Annie said, trying to avoid giving them too many details.

"The good luck charm?" Jessica said, puzzled. "Kate, you said that didn't mean anything."

"It doesn't," Kate said quickly. Then she saw the

look on Annie's face. "At least it doesn't mean anything bad," she added.

"I don't get it," Tara said. "She got kicked out because Principal Browning doesn't like her necklace? Please, if bad fashion choices are a reason to get suspended there are girls here who should have been booted out long ago."

Just then the bell for first period rang.

"Time to get to class," Kate said, thankful for the diversion. "I'll explain it to you guys at lunch."

They split up and went to their respective classes. In Spanish, Annie noticed that Sherrie once again acted as if she wasn't even there. After days of the same behavior she was getting used to it, but she couldn't shake the feeling that Sherrie was just gearing up for something later on. She had more immediate problems, though, and those were the ones she concentrated on.

All day long, everywhere she went, she heard people talking about Cooper. Some of them, miraculously, actually had the story of her suspension straight. Most of them, though, had either heard or made up a warped version of the events and were only too happy to pass them along as the truth.

"I guess she told Mrs. Browning that she'd put some kind of curse on her," Annie overheard someone telling a friend in the hallway. "They found all kinds of weird stuff in her locker, too."

"I heard she'd made a list of people she wanted to do stuff to," someone else said while Annie was walking into a classroom, but he stopped talking when he saw Annie glaring at him.

While most people talked about Cooper and what she was supposed to have done behind Annie's back, others were more direct. At lunch, while she was sitting with Sasha, two girls from the varsity cheerleading team came over. Annie recognized them as two of the girls she had done Tarot readings for the previous semester.

"Hey, Deb. Hey, Kim," she said pleasantly.

The two girls looked around anxiously without returning her greeting. "We just need to know something," Deb said. "Are you like your friend Cooper?"

"What do you mean?" Annie asked them.

"You know—are you into witchcraft? Is that why you were able to do the stuff with the cards?"

Annie looked at Sasha, who had stopped eating and was watching her expectantly. "Why do you ask that?" Annie said.

"People are saying your friend is a witch," said Kim, looking like she didn't want anyone to see her talking to Annie. "We were just wondering if you are, too."

"Cooper's not a witch," said Annie hesitantly.

"Isn't that why she got kicked out?" Deb argued.

Annie shook her head. "She got kicked out for wearing a symbol associated with witchcraft."

"But why would she wear it if she's not a witch?" pressed Deb.

"Why are you asking me all these questions?" Annie said, dodging the question.

"If you guys are witches, we were just wondering if you can do spells," Kim said. "You know, to make people fall in love and stuff."

Annie groaned. "No one around here is a witch," she said. "Sorry."

Deb and Kim looked at her skeptically for a moment. Then they walked off, looking back at her over their shoulders and talking to one another.

"That wasn't really true, you know," Sasha said when the girls were gone.

"Technically, it was," retorted Annie. "None of us are really witches yet. We're just studying it."

"But you *can* do spells," said Sasha stubbornly. "Aren't you doing what you said you wouldn't do— denying being into Wicca?"

Annie looked at her half-eaten peanut butter and strawberry jam sandwich. Suddenly she wasn't very hungry.

"You're right," she said. "I should have told them the truth. This is harder than I thought it would be."

She sat for a minute staring at the remains of her sandwich and not saying anything.

"What are you thinking?" asked Sasha.

Annie looked up. "I'm thinking it's time to do what I thought of doing yesterday," she said, standing up. "I'll see you later."

"Where are you going?" asked Sasha.

"To the library," Annie replied. "I have an article to write."

She left the cafeteria and walked to the library, where she found an empty table in the back and sat down. Taking out her notebook, she opened it to a blank page. Then, using her father's pen that she had blessed in the ritual, she started writing. She wrote quickly, and twenty minutes later she put down her pen and looked at what she'd done. There were lots of crossed-out words and arrows moving things around, but basically she was done. She read what she'd written.

> Today a friend of mine was suspended from school for refusing to stop wearing a symbol that means a great deal to her. This symbol, a pentagram, or five-pointed star, represents the fivefold path of Wicca, or witchcraft. It is an ancient symbol, and one that has long been used as a charm for protection and good luck.
>
> Unfortunately, it is also a greatly misunderstood symbol. Many people associate it with black magic and with groups involved in negative activities. My friend is not involved in any of these things. She is simply interested in the spiritual tradition of witchcraft. She wears the symbol of the pentagram because to her it is a reminder of the journey she is on.
>
> I know why this symbol is important to her

because I, too, study Wicca. To me the pentagram is a beautiful image. I'm sorry that other people have turned it into something ugly. But I don't think those of us who know its true meaning and want to celebrate that should be punished because some people are afraid of what the pentagram means.

I wanted to work on this newspaper because I believe that we need a place where we can discuss issues such as this. I hope that this editorial will start just such a discussion, not necessarily about Wicca but about freedom of speech and freedom of expression. My friend is being punished because she dared to let people know what she stands for. Well, I stand for the same things. Will I be suspended, too, because I've spoken out? I hope not. But if I am, then it's a price I'm willing to pay.

Annie Crandall
Assistant Editor

It was good, she thought. It was short and to the point, which is what Mr. Barrows had told them good journalism should be. *Now if I can just get him to run it*, she thought as the bell rang and she shut her notebook.

CHAPTER 7

"She did what?" Stephen Rivers asked his daughter.

"She suspended me," Cooper repeated. She had just finished telling her father what had happened with Mrs. Browning at school that morning. Her mother, who had already heard the story from Mrs. Browning, ate her spaghetti and didn't say anything as Mr. Rivers questioned Cooper.

"She suspended you for wearing a necklace?" he asked in disbelief, sounding like the lawyer he was.

Cooper nodded. "She said that it creates a threatening environment for some of the other students."

"That's absurd," Mr. Rivers said.

"I'm just telling you what she said," replied Cooper.

"They can't tell you what you can and cannot wear," her father said, pointing at her with his fork.

"Sure they can," said Janet Rivers, interrupting. "It's called a dress code. We have one at the lower school. Kids can't wear T-shirts with violent sayings or negative images, for example."

"That's different," her husband argued. "Cooper's necklace isn't a statement about anything. It's a symbol."

"Yes," Cooper's mother said. "But to some people that symbol is negative."

Mr. Rivers snorted. "There's always going to be someone who finds a symbol offensive," he said. "Some people find the flag offensive, for heaven's sake. But we have freedom of expression laws in this country."

Mrs. Rivers sighed. "That's easy for you to say," she answered. "You don't have to work with kids. A school does not work the same way as a democracy does. I can assure you that, freedom of expression laws or not, young people can get really excited about things like this. We have these dress codes as one way of trying to maintain some order in the school. If every kid who had something to say said it, it would result in chaos."

"But my pentacle doesn't tell anyone to do anything," said Cooper. "It's not like I'm wearing a big pin that says DOWN WITH THE POLICE or something."

"I know that," replied her mother. "But you have to understand that to some people that pentacle is very, very threatening. Some people might see the one you're wearing and think you're dangerous, too."

"Cooper's not responsible if people misunderstand the necklace," Mr. Rivers said, once again sounding like a lawyer. "Nor is she responsible for anyone else's actions."

"I didn't say it was fair, or even that it was right," said Mrs. Rivers. "I'm just trying to explain to you why schools have to maintain some control over what goes on there. When Cooper isn't on school grounds she can wear whatever she wants to. But as long as she's there she has to obey the rules."

"But it's an arbitrary rule!" Cooper told her. "It didn't even exist until yesterday, when Mrs. Greeley went in and complained."

"Be that as it may," said her mother, "it's a rule now and you have to abide by it."

Cooper looked down at her plate. She wished she could make her mother understand why this was important to her. She understood about needing to keep things at school running smoothly. But telling her not to wear a pentacle just wasn't the same as telling her not to wear clothing with offensive messages or gang-related images or something. It just wasn't.

"Tell you what," Mr. Rivers said. "Tomorrow we'll go in and have a talk with Principal Browning. I'm sure we can work this out."

"Okay," Cooper said, picking at her salad. "If you think it will help."

Mrs. Rivers sighed. "I think you should just forget about it," she said. "It's not worth it."

"Not to you, maybe," Cooper said. "But it is to me."

She looked at her mother across the table. She

81

knew her mother had issues with her involvement in witchcraft. Lots of issues, all stemming from Mrs. Rivers's own mother's interest in magic. She thought it was dangerous, and she herself had turned her back on the Craft as a young woman. She and Cooper had been through this before and had managed to come to an uneasy truce about the subject.

"I'm just going to *talk* to her," Mr. Rivers assured his wife. "That's all."

Mrs. Rivers didn't answer. She continued eating in silence, as did the rest of the family. When Cooper was finished she cleared the table, put the dishes in the dishwasher, and went to her room. She snatched her backpack from its place on the floor and went back downstairs.

"I'm going to the study group," she called to her parents, and left the house before they could answer.

When she arrived at Crones' Circle half an hour later she saw Annie and Kate already there. They were seated on cushions on the floor in the back room, talking, and they didn't look particularly happy.

"What's going on?" Cooper asked, sitting down next to them.

"I did something Kate thinks is a bad idea," Annie told her.

"You didn't wear corduroy, did you?" Cooper said, giving Annie a serious look.

"It's not funny," Kate said sharply. "She wrote an

editorial about your suspension for the *Sentinel*."

Cooper looked at Annie in surprise. "You did?" she said.

Annie nodded. "I don't know yet if they'll run it or not," she said. "Mr. Barrows is reading it, and he's going to let me know."

"So what's wrong with that?" Cooper asked Kate.

Kate sighed. "She told everyone that she's into Wicca, too," Kate said simply.

Cooper whistled. "Now I get it," she said. "Are you sure you want to do that?" she asked Annie.

"I thought about it a lot," Annie replied. "I'm tired of telling people half the truth when they ask me questions. Besides, not talking about it makes it look like we're ashamed of it." Annie looked over at Kate, who was looking at the floor. "Sorry, Kate," she said. "I didn't mean anything by that."

"Yes, you did," Kate answered. "And you're right. We *should* be able to talk about it. But you can't always do what you want to do. Look what happened to Cooper."

"But if nobody does it then it will always be this way," responded Cooper. "It's like Rosa Parks being asked to move to the back of the bus."

"This is hardly the same thing," said Kate.

"Okay, maybe it isn't," Cooper admitted. "But it sort of is. It's all about standing up for what you believe in."

"Why couldn't you just stick with saving the whales?" commented Kate unhappily.

"The whales have Greenpeace on their side," Cooper replied, trying to make Kate laugh. "So far I've just got Annie and my dad."

"Thanks a lot!" protested Annie.

Kate didn't laugh, but she did give Cooper a little smile. "What do you mean, your dad?" she asked.

"My father's going to go in tomorrow to talk to Mrs. Browning," explained Cooper.

Before she could say any more Sophia appeared and began the class. For the next hour they discussed the upcoming sabbat of Mabon, the Autumn Equinox. Cooper listened as Sophia explained the traditions and rituals of the sabbat, which, like many of the other sabbats, had traditionally been a harvest festival.

"Just as they are during the Spring Equinox, or Ostara, the hours of light and dark are equal on Mabon," Sophia told them. "But where Ostara heralds the growth of the light, we're now entering the season of darkness. The days will shorten and the sun will become weaker and weaker. This is a very important time of the year for witches. Samhain, or Halloween, is coming up, followed by Yule in December. These are two of the most meaningful and wonderful of the sabbats. It also means that for many of you your year and a day of study is almost half over."

Has it already been half a year? Cooper wondered. She counted backward in her head. Yes, the dedication ritual had been on April 12, and now it was

September 13. Five months. It was hard to believe that it had gone so quickly and that so much had happened to her and her friends. *I feel like a different person*, she thought. And it was true; she had changed a lot since first meeting Annie and Kate in February. They had all changed.

"But don't think that just because you're almost halfway there things are going to get easier." Sophia was still talking. "This is when things get *really* interesting."

The class laughed, and Cooper laughed with them. She wondered what lay ahead in the next seven months. She'd already experienced so much—communicating with a dead girl, feeling the effects of a misplaced spell, helping Sasha, meeting T.J. It seemed hard to believe that anything could top what had already happened. But if there was one thing she'd learned about Wicca and magic, it was that you could never predict what was coming next.

When class was over Cooper stayed along with Kate and Annie to help clean up. As they put chairs and cushions away and put the room back together, Sophia asked them how things were going. Cooper told her about the incident over the pentacle.

Sophia shook her head sadly. "I hate to say it, but I'm not surprised to hear about this," she said. "The Craft often comes under attack like this, especially where young people are concerned."

"Well, my father is going in to talk to the principal tomorrow," Cooper told her. "He can be pretty persuasive. I'm sure he'll work something out."

"Let me know if you need a little extra help," replied Sophia, looking up toward the sky and giving Cooper a wink. "I'll see what I can do with the lady upstairs."

The next morning Cooper sat next to her father in the chairs across the desk from Mrs. Browning. The principal was listening as Mr. Rivers spoke.

"So the way I see it, my daughter's right to express her beliefs is being impinged upon," he said, using what Cooper jokingly referred to as his courtroom voice. He wasn't arguing with the principal; he was simply explaining things to her.

"What beliefs would those be, Mr. Rivers?" asked Principal Browning.

Mr. Rivers looked at Cooper. "Her Wiccan beliefs," he said.

The principal sighed heavily. "And what would those be exactly?" she pressed.

Cooper started to speak but her father held up his hand. "What difference does it make what her beliefs are?" he said. "She has the right to express them. Let me ask you something. Are Christian students allowed to wear crosses?"

"Yes," answered Mrs. Browning. "Of course."

"And can a Jewish student wear a Star of David?"

The principal nodded. "Yes, but—" she said.

"And is a Muslim student permitted to wear a head covering?"

"I don't know that we have any Muslim students, but yes, that would be permitted," said Principal Browning.

"Then why isn't my daughter being allowed to wear a symbol of her tradition?" Mr. Rivers asked, holding up his hands as if he were completely perplexed by the situation. Inwardly, Cooper smiled, but outwardly she maintained a composed look as she waited for the principal to speak.

Mrs. Browning paused a moment, as if collecting her thoughts before speaking. "I agree with you that students with spiritual beliefs have some rights to express them as provided by law," she said slowly. "But those rights are designed to prevent religious persecution, not to allow for the expression of whatever peculiar notions a person happens to have."

"Peculiar notions?" said Cooper.

"That was a bad choice of words," the principal said. "What I mean is that those laws apply to practitioners of established religious systems."

"So just because someone belongs to a faith with a larger number of members than you think Wicca has, that means it's okay for them to wear a necklace or whatever but it's not okay for me to?" asked Cooper.

"Does Wicca have a governing body?" the principal asked in return.

Cooper shook her head. "Not that I know of."

"Does it have a principal text, like the Bible or the Koran?"

"No," Cooper replied.

"Are there buildings where you go to practice Wicca?" the principal continued.

"You don't need a building," argued Cooper defensively.

"I'm not trying to be difficult, Cooper," said Mrs. Browning. "I'm just trying to show you the situation I'm in. These are the kinds of questions I'll have to answer when concerned students or parents come to me. It's extremely difficult for me to justify your wearing that necklace as a symbol of religious expression when, from what I can see, there really isn't a lot of religion behind what you say you believe."

"We're not here to determine what my daughter does or does not believe and what the validity of those beliefs are, Principal Browning," said Cooper's father. "We're talking about a very basic right—to express one's beliefs as long as they don't interfere with the rights of other students."

"That's what I'm trying to explain to you," said the principal. "Personally, I don't have a problem with the necklace. I might not agree with Cooper's belief system, but I agree that she has a right to it. I even agree that she has the right to express her dedication to her beliefs. But what's going to happen if she continues to wear that necklace is that students and parents are going to come to me and they're going to say that they feel threatened by the necklace and what it symbolizes. Frankly, I don't see how I can justify allowing her to wear that—what do you call it again?"

"Pentacle," Cooper muttered.

"That pentacle," continued the principal, "when she can't present a convincing argument for the validity of Wicca as a genuine spiritual tradition."

Cooper looked at her father, waiting for him to counter Mrs. Browning's argument with one of his own. But he was silent, looking into the distance as if he were thinking of something else entirely. Finally, after an agonizing silence, he spoke again.

"So what you're telling me is that you're really afraid of what kind of trouble will be caused if students and their parents start complaining about this?" he asked.

"I probably wouldn't put it exactly like that, but yes," agreed the principal. "Stephen, you and I have known each other a long time. You know how I feel about the rights of young people. I wouldn't be in this position if I didn't. But you also know what kind of times we're living in. I don't just answer to myself. I answer to the parents, to the superintendent of schools, and to the school board. I have to anticipate how *they* are going to feel about this situation, and I honestly don't think they're going to be supportive. That's why I'm asking Cooper to do this now, before it becomes a real problem."

"Why don't we find out how they feel?" Mr. Rivers said.

Mrs. Browning and Cooper both looked at him.

"What do you mean?" asked the principal.

"Let's take this to the school board," said Cooper's father.

"I don't think that's a good idea," said Principal Browning.

"When's the next meeting?" asked Mr. Rivers.

The principal looked at her calendar. "Friday," she said.

"Can you get this added to the agenda?"

"I don't know," said Mrs. Browning doubtfully.

"How about if you tell them I threatened to take this to court?" asked Mr. Rivers.

Principal Browning raised an eyebrow. "You wouldn't," she said.

"You bet I would," answered Cooper's father. "The courts are all over children's rights and freedom of expression issues right now. I could have this in front of a judge in two weeks."

"In that case, I think they might be willing to hear what you have to say," said Mrs. Browning. "I'll call the president of the board and have a talk with him tonight. But if he agrees, then you'll have to be ready to make a pretty convincing argument on Friday night. They'll vote on this, and you'll need a majority to win."

"We'll get it," said Mr. Rivers confidently. "You just get it on the agenda. I'll do the rest."

He looked over at Cooper and grinned. "I told you we'd work something out," he said.

Cooper looked at Mrs. Browning and smiled. "Thanks," she said.

"Don't thank me yet," replied the principal. "This battle has just started."

"Does this mean I can come back to school?" Cooper asked.

Mrs. Browning nodded. "Sixth period is starting in ten minutes. Why don't you get to class?"

"Lunch," Cooper said brightly. "I'm there."

She stood up and started for the door. "Can I keep the pentacle on?" she asked hesitantly.

The principal looked at Mr. Rivers. "If your lawyer promises to back off, then you can wear it until the official hearing on Friday."

"Hey, Dad, back off," Cooper said with mock forcefulness.

"Whatever you say, boss," Mr. Rivers replied.

Cooper nodded. "That's what I like to hear," she said. "Especially given your exorbitant rates."

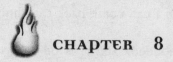

CHAPTER 8

"What did you think?"

Annie was standing in Mr. Barrows's room. She'd gotten there a little early so that she could talk to him before the other students who worked on the newspaper arrived. He had her editorial on the desk in front of him. She could see that he had written on it in a couple of places with red ink. She didn't know if that was a good sign or a bad sign.

"I like it," he said. "I think it shows a lot of passion, and it brings up an important issue."

Annie smiled. *He likes it,* she thought happily.

"But I also think that it would cause an uproar if we ran it," he continued.

The warm feeling inside of Annie melted away as she heard him say that. She'd worked so hard on the piece, and she'd really wanted him to use it in the paper.

"This will be our first issue of the *Sentinel* this year," Mr. Barrows told her. "Usually we start off with pieces about the upcoming dances and which clubs are doing what. You know: 'The French society will be holding a fudge sale,' kind of stuff. This is a lot heavier than what we normally do."

"But isn't that sort of the point of having a paper?" asked Annie. "I mean, isn't it supposed to be a place where students can talk about what's going on in their lives?"

Mr. Barrows smiled. "Spoken like a true newspaper person," he said. "Are you sure this is the first time you've worked on a paper?"

"So if that's what we're here for, why aren't you running my piece?" Annie answered.

"Who said I wasn't running it?" her teacher asked.

"Then you are?" Annie said, feeling good again.

"That depends," Mr. Barrows told her.

"On what?" asked Annie, feeling as if her emotions were being taken on a roller coaster ride.

"On you," came the response.

"Me?" said Annie. "Why on me?"

"Do *you* really want it to run?" Mr. Barrows queried.

"I wrote it, didn't I?" replied Annie.

"Yes," said Mr. Barrows. "But writing it is only the first part. It's what happens after people read it that you need to consider. Are you ready for all of the questions that are sure to come at you? Are you ready for people who don't know you to talk about you?"

"They already do that," Annie informed him.

"And yes, I'm ready for all of that."

"Then if you're sure about it, we'll put it in next week's edition. It will come out Monday."

Annie practically hugged him, she was so excited. "This is perfect," she said. "Cooper is going in front of the school board on Friday to argue her case. I know people will be talking about that on Monday. Then they'll see my piece as well. There won't be any way for them *not* to notice this. Thank you so much."

"You might want to save that thanks until you see what the response to your piece is," Mr. Barrows told her.

Annie couldn't wait to tell her friends that her editorial was going to be in the paper. She got her chance while they were all walking home together.

"So it will come out Monday morning," she said excitedly after recounting her conversation with Mr. Barrows.

"If Cooper wins on Friday it sort of won't matter, will it?" asked Kate.

Annie shrugged. "It will still get people talking," she said.

"That's for sure," said T.J. He was walking with Cooper, holding her hand. He seemed to have calmed down a little since hearing about her suspension, but Annie thought he was still acting kind of withdrawn.

"So how are things with Brian?" asked Sasha.

"I actually haven't seen much of him," Annie

told her. "I've been so busy. But we're going out tonight, so I'll see him then."

"What does he think about all of this witch stuff?" T.J. asked her suddenly.

Annie looked at Cooper and Kate. "I haven't talked to him about it," she told T.J.

"But I'm sure he'll be fully supportive," Cooper said brightly, giving T.J. a kiss on the cheek. "Just like you are."

"Not to poke a sleeping dog or anything," Kate said, "but you do seem a lot cooler about this than you did yesterday, T.J."

"Yeah, well, I kind of took out my frustrations on the punching bag my brothers set up in the basement a few years ago," he said. "Nothing like pounding a big bag of sand to help a guy get over something."

"How very butch of you," Sasha commented. "Next thing you know you'll be chopping wood."

"Doubtful," T.J. replied, playfully kicking her in the butt. "We have gas heat."

"I forgot to ask, how did your little talk with Jessica and Tara go?" Annie asked Kate, suddenly remembering that Kate had promised to fill those two in on the details of Cooper's suspension and the exact meaning of her pentacle.

"Not quite as well as T.J.'s boxing catharsis," Kate answered. "I tried explaining it to them but it just kept coming out wrong. I guess I was dancing around the subject too much."

"Again," Cooper said meaningfully.

"Give her a break," T.J. told his girlfriend. "She's trying. Not everyone's as good at being a poster child for witchcraft as you are."

"Well, on Monday I guarantee those two will have a lot more questions than they have now," Cooper said. "You'd better figure out how you're going to answer them."

"Tell me about it," Kate said under her breath.

They reached the point where they all went separate ways, and said their good-byes. Annie walked home with a spring in her step. She was going to have something published! Sure, it was just in the school newspaper. It wasn't like it was in a big magazine, or even a local paper or anything. But it was her words, and that made her feel proud of herself. She wished her parents could read it. *But at least Aunt Sarah and Meg will*, she thought happily. She wasn't going to tell them about it yet. She was going to surprise them with it on Monday, when she'd bring the paper home for them to see.

When she got home she found her aunt and her sister in the kitchen.

"Hey there," Aunt Sarah said. "How was your day?"

"Eventful," Annie said mysteriously, unable to resist.

Her aunt looked at Meg. "What do you want to bet she's not going to tell us what happened?"

"Maybe you should threaten to send her to bed

without any supper if she doesn't," said Meg. "Like Max in *Where the Wild Things Are*."

"Hmm," Aunt Sarah said, pretending to consider the suggestion. "Do you think it would work?"

"No," Meg said firmly. "But maybe you should do it anyway."

"Thanks a lot," Annie told her little sister. "But for your information I'm having dinner with Brian tonight anyway. We're going for pizza. But I'll be back early. I have a lot of homework."

"I want to come!" Meg said instantly.

"Uh-huh," Annie said, shaking her head. "Not after you tried to send me to my room."

Meg laughed, and Annie tousled her little sister's hair. "I'm going to go get dressed," Annie said, heading for the stairs that led to her room.

"You're already dressed," Meg pointed out sensibly.

"I'm going to go get dressed in something *better*," Annie clarified.

She went to her room, removed her school clothes, and opened her closet. What should she wear? she wondered. She'd recently purchased quite a lot of new clothes, many of which she hadn't even worn. She looked through them, trying to select something she thought Brian might like. Finally she settled on a pair of black jeans and a powder blue sweater set. *Simple yet elegant*, she thought as she pulled the clothes on. After putting her shoes on she went back downstairs, said good-bye to Aunt Sarah and

Meg, and went to meet Brian in town.

When she walked into the pizza parlor she saw Brian sitting in a booth. He waved at her and she walked over, sliding in across from him.

"I hope you don't mind, but I already ordered," he said. "I remember you said you liked pepperoni and extra cheese, so that's what I got."

"Perfect," Annie told him. Although she was thrilled to be having dinner with Brian, she was a little nervous. She wanted to talk to him about the situation with Cooper, and about her own involvement in Wicca, before he read about it in the paper.

"Hey," Brian said before she could begin a conversation. "We got some free tickets at the store to the Cassandra Wilson concert at the university next month. She's the singer whose CD I got you to buy, remember?"

"How could I forget?" Annie answered. The CD had quickly become one of her favorites, and not just because it had been the result of her meeting Brian at the record store where he worked.

"They're ours if we want them," he told her. "Interested?"

"Do you even have to ask?" replied Annie. "Of course I want to go."

Brian reached out and took her hand. "I can't tell you how glad I am we met," he said. "It's made being new here a lot easier. I just wish we saw each other more often in school."

"Then you'd get sick of me," said Annie.

Brian shook his head. "I don't think I could ever get sick of you," he said.

Annie knew she was blushing. She wasn't used to hearing a guy say nice things to her. Sometimes being with Brian still seemed like a wonderful dream, and she was afraid she'd wake up and find out it had all been in her imagination. He was pretty much everything she'd ever hoped for in a potential boyfriend—fun to be with, smart, and just a nice guy. It didn't hurt that he was easy to look at either.

"Um, I want to talk to you about something," she said, deciding that the time was right for the conversation she knew they needed to have.

"Uh-oh," Brian said. "Nothing good ever started with those words."

Annie laughed. "No," she said. "It's nothing bad. I just want to talk to you about Cooper."

"I saw her back in school this afternoon," said Brian. "I guess that thing about her good luck charm was cleared up, right?"

"Not yet," Annie said. "That's what I want to talk to you about."

Brian looked puzzled. Annie knew he must be wondering what Cooper's suspension had to do with him. She searched for the right words.

"Cooper is going to go before the school board on Friday," she said. "She's going to argue that she should be able to wear her necklace."

"Okay," said Brian. "But I still don't see what the big deal about it is."

Annie leaned back in the booth. "This is about more than just the necklace," she said. "See, that symbol she wears is more than just a good luck charm."

Brian studied Annie's face. "What is it, then?" he asked.

"It's called a pentagram," explained Annie. "It's a symbol used in Wicca. Do you know what that is?"

"Wicca," Brian repeated. "Not really, no."

"It's another name for witchcraft," said Annie. "Some people like to say it's the official name, but that's not really right either. Wicca is a kind of witchcraft, actually, although most people think the words mean the same thing."

"Cooper is a witch?" Brian asked, laughing. "Is she a good witch or a bad witch?"

Annie knew he was just repeating the famous line from *The Wizard of Oz* and not really asking her a question. From his response, it was clear that he really didn't think it was possible that Cooper was a witch at all. Suddenly she realized that this was going to be harder than she'd thought.

"No," she said. "Cooper isn't a witch. But she *is* studying Wicca. That's why she wears that necklace."

Brian looked at her. "You're kidding, right?"

Annie shook her head. "No," she said. "I'm not."

Brian leaned back and looked at Annie with an expression of puzzlement mixed with disbelief. "Come on," he said. "There are no witches nowadays. That's just stuff from fairy tales and movies."

Annie swallowed before she spoke. "Actually," she said, "there are a lot of witches today. You probably just don't know it because you've never met one, or at least think you haven't."

"And you're telling me your friend is studying to be one?" Brian said. "Are you serious? You're sure she hasn't been reading too many of those Harry Potter books or something?"

The conversation wasn't going the way she'd hoped it would. Brian didn't seem to even want to acknowledge that witches might be real, let alone that he was dating someone who was probably going to be one in a matter of months. Annie hadn't planned on this kind of reaction from him, and she wasn't sure how she should proceed.

"Why are you telling me all of this anyway?" Brian said before she could start speaking again.

Oh, boy, Annie thought. *Here we go.* This was the part where she was supposed to tell him how she was studying Wicca, too, and how she hoped he would understand that. But if he didn't believe that Cooper was involved in the Craft, what would he think if Annie said that *she* was? *He'd probably think you were nuts,* she told herself.

"I wrote an editorial for the school paper about Cooper's being suspended," Annie said instead. "Well, it's really about the issue of free speech. It's going to come out on Monday, and I thought you should know about it. People are probably going to talk about it, so I didn't want it to come as a surprise."

"That's great!" Brian said, surprising her. "I can't wait to read it. Why would you think I'd be upset by that?"

This is where you tell him about yourself, she thought. But although her mind wanted to do it, her mouth wasn't cooperating. She could imagine the words in her head, but she couldn't get her lips to form them. What had seemed like such a good thing to do when she'd gone over it in her head was turning out to be a lot harder in practice. *Now I know how Kate feels*, Annie realized. Thinking about telling Brian that she was studying Wicca was one thing; actually telling him was altogether different.

"I just thought you should know," Annie said stupidly. "That way, if anyone says anything about it—or about me—you'll know what it's about."

"I'm sure all they'll be saying is what a brilliant writer you are," said Brian reassuringly.

Annie smiled, feeling like a total failure. She was thankful that the waitress came with their pizza at that moment and she didn't have to say anything else, at least not immediately. She busied herself with a slice, concentrating on pulling the cheese off and popping it into her mouth.

"So your friend really believes this witch stuff?" Brian asked as he ate.

"Yes," said Annie. "She does." *And so do I*, she thought guiltily.

"I'll have to remember to watch my step around

her," Brian replied. "I wouldn't want her to put a curse on me or anything."

He laughed at his own joke. Annie laughed, too, feeling like a gigantic traitor. *Just tell him!* the voice in her head screamed. She knew Brian wasn't making jokes about Cooper because he was a mean person. He just didn't understand that to her—and to Annie and a lot of other people—witchcraft was very real. How could she make him understand that? *Correction*, she thought. *How can you make him understand that without losing him?*

"Well, whatever," said Brian. "She can think whatever she wants to. I'm not dating her, right? I'm dating you."

So much for that idea, Annie thought miserably.

"Right," she said.

She couldn't believe it. She had chickened out. Here she'd been telling Kate how *she* had to be more honest with the people in her life and she couldn't even do it herself. What was wrong with her? She'd never been shy about speaking her mind. Why couldn't she tell Brian about her involvement in the Craft? He was going to read about it in the paper on Monday anyway. She was just putting off the inevitable.

I'll tell him, she assured herself. *Right after dinner.*

CHAPTER 9

"Now that we've heard Coach Richmond's report, we need to vote on the motion to allocate funds for the purchase of new football uniforms," Mr. Dunford said. "All in favor?"

Six hands went up. Mr. Dunford looked at who they belonged to and made a note on the paper in front of him.

"That's six ayes and one nay," he said. "The motion passes, with Allison Chisolm voting against."

Cooper looked at the four men and three women sitting at the long table at the head of the room. She'd never been to a school board meeting before. If she hadn't had a personal stake in the session she would probably have fallen asleep from sheer boredom. In the hour that had elapsed since she and her father had arrived, the board had talked about a series of mundane topics, from how much to increase the head janitor's salary to whether they should paint the girls' rest rooms off-white or blue.

Aside from Cooper and her father, there were

only a couple of other people in the room. Most of them were there because they had something to say about the various issues. Principal Browning was seated in a folding chair a few rows ahead of Cooper and her dad. She'd smiled at Cooper when they'd come in but hadn't talked to them. Cooper guessed she was trying to show that she wasn't favoring one side over the other in the discussion that was about to come.

"This is worse than going to the ballet," Cooper's father whispered.

Cooper stifled a laugh. She studied the seven school board members. Some she knew, but she was seeing others for the first time. The ones she'd met before were Allison Chisolm, Jacob Weingarten, Ellen Tracy, and Marty Dunford. Allison Chisolm, who had just voted against buying new football uniforms, ran a yoga center and health spa in town. Cooper had gone there a couple of times for classes. She knew Jacob Weingarten as Professor Weingarten. He taught philosophy at Jasper College, and he'd come to some of her parents' parties. He was a strange man, and she seldom understood what he was talking about, but she liked him. Ellen Tracy was the mother of Gregory Tracy, one of Cooper's classmates. And Marty Dunford, the board president, ran one of the town's most popular hardware stores.

She'd never met the other three members before. Constance Reeder was an older woman with a serious expression. She listened carefully to everything that was said, took notes, and nodded a lot. Hector Alvarado was a local businessman who, her father told her, ran a printing company in town. The final member of the board was someone Cooper wasn't in any hurry to be introduced to. She'd never met Ralph Adams in person, but she was sure that they wouldn't get along. For one thing, he looked mean. He looked as if he'd never smiled in his life. He sat behind the table with his arms folded across his chest, glaring at everyone. That alone was enough to make Cooper want to steer clear of him. But even worse, he was the father of Sherrie Adams, which to Cooper instantly put him in the category of enemy.

Her father had explained to her before they arrived that the board would ask to hear arguments from both sides, which in this particular case was Cooper and Principal Browning. The board members would then debate the issue among themselves and decide what to do. It seemed straightforward enough to Cooper, but she didn't know what the outcome would be. She knew that secretly Mrs. Browning was on her side, but the principal had already made it clear that whatever her personal feelings about the matter were she had to consider the feelings of the other students and their parents.

"Okay," Marty Dunford said. "We have one final piece of new business, then. This is the question Principal Browning has brought before us about the right of a student to wear a potentially offensive symbol. Principal Browning, would you like to tell us what this is all about?"

The principal stood up. "Recently one of our students, Cooper Rivers, began wearing a necklace to school that features a symbol that other students find unsettling," Mrs. Browning said. "After one teacher and several students and their parents expressed their concerns to me, I asked Miss Rivers to stop wearing the necklace. She refused. I informed her that her refusal to comply with my request would result in suspension. She chose suspension. Then, after a meeting with her and her father, I suggested that we bring the matter before the board."

Principal Browning sat down. Marty Dunford nodded and looked at Cooper. "Is that what happened, Miss Rivers?" he asked.

Cooper stood up, as did her father. "Yes," Cooper said simply.

"And just what is this symbol you've been wearing?" Mr. Dunford asked.

"It's called a pentagram," Cooper explained. She walked toward the table where the board was sitting and held out her hand to Mr. Dunford. She'd removed her necklace at the suggestion of her father, and now she handed it to the board president to look at.

"As you can see, it's a five-pointed star," Cooper said as Mr. Dunford looked at it and then passed it to Mrs. Reeder.

"And does it have some meaning?" asked Ms. Chisolm, who was examining the necklace as it was passed to her.

Cooper swallowed. This was the part she and her father had gone over numerous times during the days before the meeting. "It represents the four elements: earth, air, fire, and water," Cooper said. "The fifth point represents spirit."

"I don't see how that could be offensive," Ms. Chisolm said as she handed the pentacle to Mr. Alvarado.

Cooper didn't respond. Her father had told her not to bring up the connection between the pentagram and Wicca until she had to. Then Mrs. Browning stood up again.

"The pentagram is a symbol associated with witchcraft," she said, sounding as if she really didn't want to tell the board that information. "Some people also associate it with black magic or Satanism. Seeing Miss Rivers wearing it upset several students."

Professor Weingarten had taken the pentacle and was peering at it closely over his glasses. He looked at Cooper and smiled, which made her feel slightly more relaxed. "I hardly think Miss Rivers is advocating devil worship, are you, Miss Rivers?"

"No," Cooper said.

"Then why wear something associated with it?" asked Mrs. Tracy, who was holding the pentacle by the cord and not touching it as she looked at it.

"I don't associate it with those things," Cooper said calmly. "Other people do."

"I still don't understand," Mrs. Tracy replied. "What *do* you associate it with?"

"With Wicca," Cooper said reluctantly.

"Wicca?" Mr. Dunford said. "What's that?"

Mr. Rivers stepped to his daughter's side. "Wicca is a spiritual tradition," he explained. "It's a nature-based religion."

"Religion?" Mr. Alavardo repeated, sounding skeptical. "How come I've never heard of it?"

"Many people haven't," Mr. Rivers explained. "I myself hadn't until Cooper educated me."

"Do you approve of your daughter's wearing this symbol, Mr. Rivers?" asked Mrs. Reeder.

Cooper's father nodded. "Yes," he said. "It's something that's important to her, and I see nothing wrong with it."

"But Principal Browning says that she's had some complaints about it," Mr. Dunford said.

"Yes," Mrs. Browning said. "Several. People are concerned that seeing the symbol is distracting and upsetting to some students, even though to Cooper I'm sure its meaning is entirely positive."

Mr. Dunford nodded. "What do you all think?" he asked the other members of the board.

"I don't see anything at all wrong with it," Professor Weingarten said instantly. "I think that if it genuinely means something to Miss Rivers she should be allowed to wear it."

"What if she wanted to wear a Nazi swastika?"

Cooper looked to see who had asked the question. It was Ralph Adams. He was holding her pentacle and looking at Mr. Weingarten.

"But it isn't a swastika," the professor protested.

"What if it was?" Mr. Adams asked doggedly. "What if she wanted to wear a necklace with a swastika on it? Would that bother you?"

"Yes, it would bother me," Professor Weingarten answered. "I lost many relatives to the Nazis in the war. It would upset me to see someone wearing a symbol associated with them."

"But the swastika wasn't always a Nazi symbol," said Mr. Adams. "It's actually a Hindu religious symbol meaning 'let good prevail.'"

"But that's not what people see it as today," said the professor.

"Exactly," said Mr. Adams, smiling for the first time. "So it's not what it *really* means that's important, it's what people *think* it means. If people see this pentagram and think of black magic and Satanism, it doesn't really matter if it actually stands for this Wicca stuff. Do you see what I'm saying?"

Mr. Weingarten nodded reluctantly. "I understand," he said. "But I don't think this is the same thing."

"Why not?" Ellen Tracy asked. "We would never let a student wear a swastika because it might offend other students. Why should Miss Rivers be allowed to wear a symbol that frightens or angers other students?"

"We see this as a matter of both freedom of speech and freedom of religious expression," Mr. Rivers said quickly before anyone else could speak.

"Excuse me for saying so," said Mr. Alvarado, "but if I've never heard of Wicca I bet a lot of people haven't. It's hard for me to accept that it's a religion like, say, Judaism or Islam."

"And even if this is a religious symbol," Mrs. Reeder said, "that doesn't necessarily protect it as far as wearing it in school is concerned."

Cooper looked at her father. He had a strained expression, and she knew he was angry and trying not to show it. She was angry, too. Some of the board members were talking as if Wicca were some kind of joke instead of a real thing. Even Professor Weingarten, who had seemed to be her strongest supporter, had backed down. *Thanks to Sherrie's dad*, Cooper thought bitterly. If it hadn't been for what Mr. Adams had said about the swastika, no one would have thought of that. But he had brought it up, and now he seemed very pleased with himself. He was looking at Cooper with almost a look of triumph in his eyes. Cooper wondered just what he knew about her. Whatever it was, it was probably lies made up by his daughter.

"I understand about protecting students from being offended," Ms. Chisolm said forcefully. "I know I don't like to see things that I disagree with either. But don't you think we're maybe underestimating them here?"

"What do you mean, Allison?" asked Mrs. Tracy.

"We're saying that we have to protect them from this symbol," said the other woman. "But how are they going to learn what different people think or believe if we keep them in this sterile little cocoon?"

"Why *should* they learn about it?" Mr. Adams barked.

"So they learn to be more tolerant," answered Ms. Chisolm pointedly.

"I don't think having some students parading around in witchcraft symbols is going to teach tolerance," Mr. Adams said derisively. "It just teaches them that anything goes."

Cooper wanted to scream at him. Actually, she wanted to slap him. But she stood in place, clenching her fists so that the nails dug into her palms. Mr. Adams was railroading the board, and he knew it. She could tell that he didn't know the first thing about witchcraft or what it was. He was simply being a jerk. *Just like those judges who presided over the witchcraft trials during the Inquisition and at Salem Village*, she thought. *I bet he'd like to see me burned at the stake, too.*

While everyone was talking, Mr. Dunford had been looking at a small book that sat on the table next to him. Now he held up his hand. "According to the official school bylaws," he said, reading from the book, "'No student may wear clothing or jewelry featuring gang symbols, offensive words or messages, images promoting sexism, racism, homophobia, or other kinds of bias, or images or wording that may cause other students to feel unsafe or uncomfortable in the school environment.' We adopted that definition two years ago after one of the senior boys wore a shirt with a Confederate flag on it and several students complained that it was associated with racist causes."

He shut the book and looked at the other board members. "I agree with Jacob that I don't think Cooper means anything negative by wearing this necklace," he said. "But if we banned the Confederate flag because it made kids uncomfortable I think this might fall into the same category."

"But the Confederate flag is not a religious symbol," reasoned Mr. Rivers. "What about Cooper's right to practice her religion?"

"You haven't convinced me that this *is* a real religion," Mr. Alvarado said. "Personally, I don't think that it is, so I don't see how we can justify letting your daughter wear this necklace."

"If it's a symbol of witchcraft I don't think it should be allowed anyway," added Mrs. Tracy. "Kids come to school to learn reading, writing, math, science, and history. Real subjects. They don't come to learn about witchcraft. I don't want *my* child being exposed to that, even if some parents think it's acceptable."

She gave Cooper's father a long look as she

spoke. Cooper knew what she was thinking. Her father was a bad parent for letting her experiment with Wicca. She knew that's what Mrs. Tracy would call it, experimenting. *She's so narrow-minded her head could slip through a mail slot*, Cooper thought.

"I think we should vote," Mr. Dunford said. "I guess the motion will be to uphold Principal Browning's decision to ban the wearing of pentacles at Beecher Falls High School. All in favor?"

Mrs. Tracy, Mr. Alvarado, Mrs. Reeder, and Mr. Dunford all raised their hands. Mr. Adams was the last to put his in the air, and Cooper couldn't help but think that it was more like he was raising his fist in triumph.

"All against?" said Mr. Dunford.

Professor Weingarten and Ms. Chisolm raised their hands.

"You're just voting against everything tonight, aren't you, Allison?" Mr. Dunford said jovially as he wrote down their votes in his notebook. Then he looked up at Cooper. "The motion has passed," he said. "I'm sorry, Miss Rivers, but you'll have to stop wearing this necklace."

"Or what?" asked Cooper defiantly.

"Or else you can't come back to school," said Mr. Dunford sadly.

Cooper snorted. "That's it?" she said. "You guys get to decide and no one else gets to have a say?"

The board looked at her in surprise. She stared back at them, daring them to say something. She was in a fighting mood, and she was ready to take on anyone and everyone. As she looked at each of their faces she saw that Ms. Chisolm was smiling slightly while the others either looked away or glared at her with open hostility for daring to speak to them in such a manner.

"You can always request a revote," Mr. Dunford said finally. "But in order to do that you need a petition signed by at least one hundred and fifty students in support of your request. If you can get that, then we'll rehear your case, along with any new evidence you have to support your argument, and we'll revote."

Like any of you are going to change your minds, she thought, but what she said was, "When's the next meeting?"

Mr. Dunford looked at his notes. "Friday, September the thirtieth," he said.

"That doesn't give you much time," her father said, leaning over to whisper so that the board couldn't hear their conversation. "I say we threaten them with a lawsuit."

"Not yet," Cooper replied. "I want to do this my way."

Her father smiled at her and nodded. Cooper knew he was proud of her for standing up to the board on her own.

"Fine," she said to Mr. Dunford. "I'll get that petition. Thank you for your time. May I have my pentacle back now?"

She walked briskly to the table, held out her

hand, and took the necklace from Mr. Dunford. As the board watched she put it around her neck and knotted the cord in the back.

"Please be aware that you cannot wear that necklace to school until this is decided once and for all," Mr. Dunford reminded her.

Cooper didn't answer. She turned and walked back to where her father stood.

"I guess this meeting is adjourned, then," Mr. Dunford said. "I'll see you all on the thirtieth."

"Well, it wasn't what we were hoping for," Mr. Rivers said to Cooper.

"No," Cooper answered. "But it's not over yet."

She and her father turned to leave the room. As they did, Cooper saw a familiar figure stand up and walk toward them. She groaned.

"What is that nosy reporter doing here?" Cooper said.

Amanda Barclay walked over to Cooper and her father. She was smiling broadly. "Hello, Cooper," she said.

Cooper nodded in reply. She didn't have anything to say to Amanda, who wrote for one of the local papers. It had been Amanda who had leaked the story about Cooper's helping the police solve the disappearance and murder of Elizabeth Sanger, a local girl, earlier in the year. In the process she had also almost cost an innocent man his life by reporting false facts about his involvement in the crime. Cooper had no love for Amanda and had hoped she would never see her again. But now the reporter was standing in front of her, the familiar fake smile plastered to her face.

"What can we do for you, Ms. Barclay?" asked Mr. Rivers.

Cooper noted with some satisfaction that her father seemed as uninterested in talking to the reporter as she was. Before everything that had happened surrounding the death of Elizabeth Sanger, Stephen Rivers had been a huge fan of Amanda's writing. Now, though, he seemed to see her for what she really was.

Amanda ignored the coldness of his response. "I've been covering local politics for the paper," said Amanda. "That's why I'm here."

"You mean you were given the school board beat when you got in trouble at the paper for writing those bogus stories," Cooper said.

She could tell from the brief lapse in Amanda's smile that she was right. But the reporter quickly regained her composure.

"I write about what's going on in the schools and in city government," she said. "I think we have a great story here."

Cooper sniffed. "Right," she said.

"No," Amanda said. "I really do. Your dad is right—this is a case about freedom of speech and freedom of religion. I'd like to write about it."

"You don't know anything about Wicca," Cooper said. "You'd just make up a lot of nonsense to try and be sensational."

Amanda shook her head. "No," she said. "I really want to write about this. And if you help me, we can put something great together."

Cooper looked at the reporter. She didn't trust her. But getting some coverage for her case in the local paper might not be a bad idea. She needed to influence people's opinions if she was going to have a chance of winning. If only she could get someone other than Amanda to do it.

"I don't know," she said hesitantly.

"Would you promise to let us see everything you write before it goes to print?" Mr. Rivers asked.

"Absolutely," Amanda said. "Every word. I'm serious when I say that I want to do a good job on this. I really do think it's an important topic."

Mr. Rivers looked at Cooper. "What do you think?" he asked.

The members of the school board were walking past them as they left the room. Most of them avoided looking at Cooper as they went by. But Ralph Adams looked right at her, and on his face Cooper saw an expression of disdain. It was people like Ralph Adams she wanted to show up.

"Okay," she said to Amanda. "Let's talk."

CHAPTER 10

"Where is it?" Annie asked Kate and Cooper anxiously.

"Let me at least open it," said Kate as she flipped over the first few pages of the *Sentinel*. The girls scanned each page, looking for Annie's editorial.

"There it is," Cooper said, pointing.

Annie's column took up the left-hand side of page 3. The three friends stood reading it as other students walked by on their way to classes. Annie looked up and was both anxious and thrilled to see that a lot of other people had grabbed copies of the school paper from the stack by the front door and were reading them.

"It's great," Cooper told Annie when she had finished reading.

"Not as great as the piece Amanda Barclay did on you in the *Tribune* this morning," said Annie.

As promised, Amanda Barclay had indeed written an article about Cooper's run-in with the school board. Cooper couldn't even find anything in it to complain about, except perhaps for the fact that it was buried on page 17 instead of being closer to the front. Amanda had even mentioned the fact that Cooper was starting a petition to get the school board to reconsider its decision. Cooper was hoping that might make it easier for her to get signatures. She'd written up the petition with her father's help and had it in her backpack, ready for signing.

"Hey there," Sasha said, walking up to them. "How does it feel to be celebrities, you two?"

Cooper and Annie pretended to be shielding their faces from paparazzi. "Please," Cooper said breathlessly. "No pictures."

"You'll have to speak to my agent," Annie added as both of them laughed.

"Freaks," someone muttered.

The girls turned to see who had said it, but nobody was speaking to them. It could have been any of the students walking by, but since none of them actually stopped to say anything, they couldn't tell who had spoken.

"I'm afraid you're going to get a lot of that," Kate told her friends.

"Maybe for a while," said Cooper. "Then it will all blow over."

"I see you agreed not to wear the pentacle," Sasha commented to Cooper.

"Yeah," Cooper replied. "My dad said I should play nice for now, at least until we see if this revote comes off."

"Do you think you can actually get enough signatures on that petition?" asked Annie.

"We'll find out," said Cooper. "Why don't you guys be the first three to sign it."

"How about the first four?"

Cooper turned and saw T.J. standing behind her. "Did you see the article?" she asked him.

"Both of them," he said. "Good job, Annie."

"Thanks," said Annie happily.

"And what did you think of the one about me?" asked Cooper.

"You know what I think about that," answered her boyfriend. "But I'm going to be supportive and not say anything."

"Good boy," Cooper said, kissing him. "Now sign."

She handed him her petition, and he wrote his name on the first line. Then Annie, Sasha, and Kate added their names after T.J.'s.

"Only a hundred and forty-six to go," said Cooper confidently. "Then I can wave it in Ralph Adams's face. Even if they don't change their minds, it will be fun just to see him get angry."

"Oh, here comes Brian," Annie said excitedly. "Let's see what he thinks of the article."

"You didn't tell him?" Kate said.

Annie turned red. "Not exactly," she said. "I meant to, but it seemed easier this way."

She really had meant to tell Brian. She'd promised herself that she would do it right after dinner on their date Wednesday night. But somehow she'd kept putting it off, first until after dessert, then until after their walk along the beach, then until after he walked her to the bus stop. By the time she knew it she was home in bed and she still hadn't told him.

"It's not a big deal," she said confidently. "He'll be okay with it."

Brian walked up to the group. "Hi," he said.

"Hi," Annie said. "Did you see my article? The one I told you about?"

"Yeah," answered Brian. "But you didn't exactly tell me everything about it."

"What do you mean?" Annie asked, not understanding.

"You didn't tell me that you were into this . . . you know."

"Wicca?" Annie said, filling in the blank he'd left at the end of his sentence.

"Yeah," Brian said again. "That."

"I didn't think it was all that important," said Annie.

Brian didn't say anything. The others looked at him, and then at Annie, as she waited for him to speak.

"Can we talk?" Brian asked her. "Alone?"

"Sure," said Annie.

She followed Brian as he walked to the side of the hall, away from her friends.

"Look," he told her when they had a little privacy. "I really like you. But I'm just not into this kind of stuff."

"You don't have to be into it," Annie said. "I'm not asking you to be."

"But you're into it," Brian said.

Annie shook her head. "So?"

"What am I supposed to tell people, Annie?" said Brian.

"Tell them about what?" Annie asked.

Brian sighed. "People are talking," he said. "They're saying you and your friend are witches."

"And that matters why?" Annie queried.

"You want me to tell people I'm dating a witch?" said Brian. "You want me to tell my *parents* that I'm going out with this really great girl who happens to practice witchcraft? I don't think so."

"You're talking about it like it's something bad," Annie said defensively.

"Well, maybe I think it is," said Brian.

"Do you?" asked Annie.

Brian didn't respond. "I just don't think we should go out anymore," he said. "I'm sorry."

Annie couldn't believe what she was hearing. Was Brian dumping her?

"But I'm the same person I was before you knew about this," she said.

"No," Brian said. "You're not. Now you're a girl who's into something I don't really want anything to do with."

Annie stared at him. He had to be kidding. Just a few nights before they'd been holding hands and making plans for the future.

"What about the Cassandra Wilson concert?" she said dully.

"I think we should skip it," came Brian's reply.

"So that's it?" Annie asked. "I say that I'm interested in Wicca and—bang—suddenly I'm not good enough to date?"

"You're still good enough to date," Brian told her. "You're just not the kind of girl *I* want to date. It's nothing personal."

Annie laughed sharply. "Nothing personal?" she said loudly enough for people to turn around and look at her.

"I've got to go," said Brian. "Maybe we'll talk later. I'd still like to be friends."

He turned and walked away from her, leaving her speechless. She watched him go, unable to move. Kate, Cooper, and Sasha came over. Kate put her arm around Annie. "What happened?"

"He broke up with me," Annie said quietly.

"Because of the editorial?" Cooper asked. "What a jerk."

Annie shook her head. "That's the thing," she said. "He's not a jerk. He's a nice guy. But he still dumped me."

She looked at her friends, her eyes wet with the tears that were beginning to roll down her cheeks. "I think I made a mistake," she said. "I think I made a horrible mistake."

Cooper put her arm around Annie's other shoulder, so that Annie was sandwiched between her and Kate. "You didn't make a mistake," she said. "He just couldn't handle it."

"But what if other people can't handle it?" she asked, wiping her face with her hand. "I never thought Brian would turn his back on me because of this."

Kate looked at Cooper. "This is exactly what I was afraid of," she said.

"If you say I told you so I'm going to shriek," Cooper answered. "So one person freaked out. We knew this wasn't going to be totally pain free."

"Could you have maybe an ounce of sympathy here?" Kate said. "It wasn't just anyone who freaked out—it was Annie's boyfriend. And now he's dumped Annie because she tried to help you."

"I thought he would understand," Annie said numbly, as if she wasn't even listening to the conversation going on around her.

"It will be okay," Cooper said, trying to console her.

"Right," Sasha added. "And who knows, maybe Brian will come around."

The bell rang, interrupting their talk.

"Time to go," Kate said. "Come on, Annie. Sasha and I will walk with you to class."

Cooper gave Annie another hug and then left with T.J. Kate, Annie, and Sasha walked in the other direction, toward the English and Spanish classrooms. Annie didn't say a word as she trudged along between them.

"It really is a great editorial," said Sasha. "You should be proud of it."

"And you couldn't know that Brian would get freaked out," Kate added.

"I just don't get it," said Annie after a minute. "It doesn't bother Aunt Sarah. It doesn't bother Meg. It's not even an issue with them."

"That's because they know you," said Sasha. "Brian was just getting to know you. You turned out to be something different from what he thought you were. Guys are *always* freaked out by that."

"If it helps any, I know how you feel," Kate told her friend. "I know Tara and Jessica are going to read that editorial, and I'm going to have to tell them something."

"Great," Annie said. "So now you're saying that I've ruined *your* life as well as mine. That makes me feel a lot better."

"That's not what I'm saying at all," Kate said. "All I'm saying is that, for better or for worse, we're all having to deal with this issue now. It would have happened whether you wrote that editorial or not. This whole thing with Cooper and the pentacle wasn't going to go away just because we wanted it to."

"I wish she'd never bought that thing," Annie said in response.

"I can't say I haven't thought the same thing," said Kate. "But I know it's important to her, and on some level I'm glad she's doing this."

"I know," Annie said. "I guess I feel the same

way. But that doesn't make it any easier."

"No," Kate said, clearly thinking about the conversations she herself would undoubtedly be having soon. "No, it doesn't."

They reached the door to Ms. Lopez's room, and Kate and Sasha said good-bye. Annie took a deep breath to make sure she wasn't going to start crying and then went inside. As she took her seat she noticed a number of her classmates turning and looking at her.

"Great editorial, Annie," said Greta Mueller, who sat next to her.

"Thanks," said Annie. Hearing someone say that the editorial was good made her feel a little better, but not much. The fact that some people appreciated what she had to say didn't really make up for the fact that her saying it had driven Brian away.

Ms. Lopez walked into the room. *"Buenos días,"* she said. "Today we're going to go over what we discussed last week. So if you'll all turn to page twenty—"

"Ms. Lopez?"

Annie looked and saw Sherrie with her hand raised. It was the first time she'd spoken in class, and Annie wondered what she could possibly have to say.

"Yes, Sherrie?" the teacher asked.

Sherrie lowered her hand. "Before we start I just want to make a quick announcement. I'm sure a lot of you have already seen today's edition of the *Sentinel.*"

Annie felt herself tense up. Why was Sherrie talking about the newspaper?

"Some of you may have also seen the piece in the *Tribune*," continued Sherrie. "If you haven't, there's a petition going around attempting to get the school board to reverse a decision it made banning Satanic symbols from being worn in school. Well, I'm collecting signatures for another petition—one that supports the school board's decision. I just wanted to let people know that if they'd like to sign it they can see me after class."

"Thank you, Sherrie," Ms. Lopez said, her voice even and empty of any discernible emotion. "I'm not sure this class was the proper place to bring that up, but since you did, I'm sure those students who support your petition will be happy to see you when we're through."

"I'm sorry, Ms. Lopez," Sherrie said in a voice Annie felt was dripping with fake sincerity. "I just thought it was important, that's all."

Ms. Lopez ignored her and began the class. Although she feigned interest, Annie was thinking about anything but Spanish. First there was the response to her editorial to worry about. Then there was Brian's response in particular. She didn't know what to do about that. No, it was worse than that. She knew that there was nothing she *could* do about that. She couldn't pretend that she wasn't involved in the Craft. She couldn't take back what she'd written.

That's what hurt the most—knowing that she'd been open about who she was and that Brian had rejected her. *It would be easier if he just thought I was ugly,* she thought. *Or if he hated my laugh or something. It would even be easier if he thought my chest was too flat.* But up until the moment he'd read the editorial Brian *had* liked her. He had seemed to like everything about her. It was just knowing that she was into Wicca that he didn't like.

I suppose this is my punishment for doing that blue moon ritual, Annie thought, continuing with her torturous train of thought. But deep down she knew that wasn't true. She couldn't blame what had happened on any sort of karmic mishap. It was all because she had told the truth, plain and simple. She'd told the world, or at least the world of Beecher Falls High School, that she was interested in witchcraft. Now she was finding out just what people thought about that.

When class ended Annie got up and left quickly. As she exited the room she noticed that several students had remained behind to talk to Sherrie about her petition. Would they sign it? she wondered. Were people *really* afraid of what Cooper's pentacle symbolized? She couldn't believe Sherrie had dared to call it a Satanic symbol. *No,* she corrected herself. *I'm not surprised at all. That's exactly what she wants people to think.* Hadn't Cooper said that Sherrie's father had been the one to give her the most trouble at the school board meeting? The petition was probably all his idea. And Sherrie had timed her announcement perfectly—waiting until Annie was around to hear it. So, she was trying to exact revenge after all, but she was doing it not by attacking Annie directly but by trying to destroy something that was important to Annie and her friends, all of whom happened to be the people Sherrie most wanted to see hurt.

She practically ran to history. Partly she wanted to be with her friends, where she felt a little less exposed than she did walking around by herself, but she also wanted to tell them about Sherrie's latest plan. However, when she arrived at class she found them already talking about it.

"I guess this is her idea of revenge," Kate said. "How many people were signing her petition, Annie?"

Annie shook her head. "I didn't stick around to find out," she answered. "Three or four, I guess."

"I heard she already got twenty signatures," said Sasha. "How many do you have, Coop?"

"Just you guys so far," Cooper replied. "I hadn't really started yet."

"You'd better," Kate told her. "You *need* to get that petition filled up now. You can't have Sherrie showing up with more names than you have. I know her. She won't stop until she has every last student in school on her list."

"I'll get on it at lunch," said Cooper.

"Take your seats," said Mrs. Greeley, coming in and shutting the door with a bang. "This is not social hour."

Annie and her friends scattered, going to their desks and sitting. Mrs. Greeley walked to her own desk and stood looking out at the class. That's when Annie noticed that she was holding a copy of the *Sentinel* in her hands.

"It seems one of our class members has become something of a cause célèbre," the teacher said. "Or perhaps I should say two of our members." She held up a copy of the *Tribune* that was turned to the page with the article about Cooper on it. Looking at the two papers in Mrs. Greeley's hands, Annie remembered that it had been partly because of their teacher that the issue over Cooper's pentacle had been raised at all. She glanced over at Cooper, who looked back. What was Mrs. Greeley going to do? Annie wondered.

"Since Miss Crandall and Miss Rivers seem to believe that there are issues of freedom of speech involved in their crusade, I thought perhaps we could use this situation as a basis for discussing the reasons why the early colonists came to America. They, too, were searching for such freedom."

The teacher paused. Annie tried to imagine how Mrs. Greeley was possibly going to use her and Cooper in the class discussion. She didn't even *want* her to use them, but apparently it was too late for that.

Mrs. Greeley smiled. "We're going to do something a little different," she said. "We're going to have a mock trial. The focus will be on defending the notions of free speech. Miss Rivers will be the defendant. Miss Crandall will be her attorney. The prosecuting attorney will be Mr. Reynolds."

Annie looked at John Reynolds. He was grinning from ear to ear. *He* would *think this was fun*, she thought. John, she knew, planned on going to law school. This was exactly the kind of assignment he would excel at. She, on the other hand, hated speaking in public.

"You will each prepare arguments and have them ready for class a week from today," Mrs. Greeley said. "The class will be the jury, and they will decide which of you presents the stronger argument."

"And who'll be the judge?" Cooper asked.

Mrs. Greeley looked at her and smiled slowly. "Why, I will," she said.

CHAPTER II

Kate kept rolling the apple over and over in her hands. She told herself she was rubbing it clean, but she knew she was just trying to occupy herself while she waited for Jessica and Tara to arrive. She'd been tempted to skip lunch altogether, but she knew that at some point she had to face her friends and talk to them about what was going on. There was no way they wouldn't have heard about it by now, and she knew they would come running to her first for information.

"There you are," she heard Tara say. She shut her eyes and sent a silent prayer to the Goddess. *Help me make it through this.*

"Hey," she said brightly as Tara and Jessica sat down, hoping they wouldn't see that she was incredibly stressed out.

"So, what gives with Annie and Cooper?" Tara asked immediately. "They're all anybody is talking about."

"I guess they went all over the caf last period

asking people to sign that petition Cooper's got going," said Jessica. "A couple of the girls on the team signed it."

"Really?" Kate said, surprised.

"Yeah," Jessica replied. "I think it's cool what she's doing."

"You do?" asked Kate.

"Why wouldn't I?" Jessica said, unwrapping her pita bread and hummus sandwich.

"Well, the other day you said she was kind of weird because she wore that symbol," Kate said.

"No," Jessica said. "I said that *some* people thought she was weird because she wore it. I didn't really know what it was."

"We read Annie's editorial," Tara said. "I guess everybody has. Did you know they were both into this Wicca stuff?"

Kate hesitated. This was the moment she'd been thinking about all day. She looked at Jessica and Tara. They were waiting for her to answer.

"Yeah," she said. "I knew. And I knew what Cooper's pentacle meant, too. I'm sorry I pretended not to when you asked me the other day. I thought you might be freaked out."

"That's okay," Jessica said. "I guess they were trying to keep it quiet."

"There's something else," Kate said.

Her friends looked at her expectantly.

"Remember when we met that woman outside the movie theater and we told you that she runs a book group at Crones' Circle?"

Tara and Jessica nodded.

"It's not really a book group," said Kate. "It's a witchcraft study group. Cooper and Annie go to it."

Jessica's eyes went wide. "They have a *study* group for that?" she said. "Cool."

"Sign me up," Tara said, laughing. "I wonder what the homework is like? Turning people into toads, probably."

Jessica and Tara laughed as Kate continued to play with her apple, which remained uneaten.

"I go, too," she said softly.

Her friends stopped laughing and looked at her without saying anything.

"I go, too," Kate repeated, unsure if they'd heard her or not. "To the study group. I'm studying Wicca with them." She was surprised at how easy it had been to say. But how would her friends respond? she wondered, thinking about Brian and Annie.

"You?" Tara said in disbelief.

Kate was taken aback. "Why do you say it like that?" she asked, puzzled.

Tara shrugged. "It's just that you're so . . . normal. I wouldn't expect you to be into something like that."

"Well, I am," said Kate, slightly hurt. "I'm not *that* boring, you know."

Jessica leaned forward on her elbows, her sandwich in one hand. "You really go to this witch group?" she said.

Kate nodded. "For a little more than five months now," she answered.

"How did this happen?" asked Jessica.

Kate sighed. "That's a long story," she said. "A *really* long story. Can I tell you some other time?"

"Sure," Jessica said.

Kate looked at her friends. "You guys are really okay about this?" she said uncertainly.

Tara rolled her eyes. "God, you're acting like you just told us that you're going to Switzerland for gender reassignment," she said. "You're just taking a class. What's the big deal about that?"

Kate laughed. "I guess you're right," she said. "But it's more than just a class. Annie, Cooper, and I do other things, too."

"Like?" Jessica said.

Kate tried to think of the best way to explain herself. Suddenly she realized that trying to convey to other people what being involved in the Craft entailed was harder than it seemed. She couldn't really think of how to tell Jessica and Tara about the rituals she and her friends did, or about the spells they sometimes worked. It all seemed so abstract when she attempted to put it into words. So much of what practicing Wicca was about was emotional and deeply personal. Trying to sum it up in one easy explanation was impossible.

"It's something that affects my whole life," she said, feeling completely inadequate. "It's really changed how I see things. How I see myself."

"Is that why you stopped hanging around with us?" asked Jessica.

"Sort of," Kate answered. "When I first got involved I didn't really know what I was doing. Some stuff happened that was really confusing, and I couldn't tell you guys about it because I didn't really understand it myself. But then Cooper and Annie and I found this group and that has helped us a lot."

"Sounds like therapy to me." Jessica commented.

"No," Kate said. "It's just really hard to explain."

"Maybe we could come to this group sometime," said Tara.

Jessica nodded in agreement. "Right," she said. "It sounds cool."

Kate finally took a bite of her apple. She was glad that her friends weren't spazzing on her, but she wasn't sure how far to go with the conversation.

"It's not really something you just go to to see what it's like," she said. "You have to commit to it."

"Don't they have some kind of intro class or anything?" asked Jessica. "I mean, how do you know if you want to do it?"

It was a good question. Kate, Cooper, and Annie had ended up in the class almost by default. They'd jumped into the deep end of the Craft, so to speak, and had found Crones' Circle and the study group pretty much by accident. But surely there were people who went there just to learn more about Wicca.

"I'll ask," she told Jessica and Tara.

"So basically you're telling us that the three of you are witches, is that right?" Tara asked Kate.

"No," Kate said. "The study group is to find out if you want to become a witch. It's not just something you decide overnight."

"And do you?" Jessica asked. "Want to be a witch, I mean."

Kate hesitated. This was a question she herself had been thinking about a lot lately. "I'm not sure," she said. "I know that I like learning about it, and I know that it's really made me understand a lot of things about myself. But I don't know if it's something I'm going to commit to forever."

"Well, it sounds interesting," said Jessica. "So, are you signing up for basketball or not?"

It was a dramatic change in the direction of the conversation, and for a moment Kate was taken aback. Was that it? That's all her friends wanted to know about her big revelation? She'd been expecting more. A lot more. But they were treating her announcement the same way they might react to her telling them that she was getting a perm or something.

"Um, I still don't know," answered Kate. "Like I said, the study group is on Tuesdays."

"We'd really miss you if you stopped playing," Tara said. "If we can't come to this class of yours, at least it would be nice to see you on the court."

"I know," Kate said, feeling a little sad. "I want

to play. But I promised Archer and Sophia that I would stick with the class until the end. Let me think about it."

You can think about it all you want to, she told herself. *That's not going to change the night that classes are on.* What was she going to do? She knew she wouldn't give up the class, but playing ball with Jessica and Tara would be a lot of fun. Plus it would be something she could do that wasn't Wicca-related. Lately she'd been feeling as if her whole life was taken up with things having to do with the Craft.

"You know Sherrie is trying to get people to sign a petition asking for the total ban of occult symbols, right?" Tara said.

"I know," Kate replied. "Cooper said Mr. Adams was really nasty to her at the school board hearing."

"She's got a lot of kids scared," said Jessica. "She's telling them that Cooper and Annie want to start holding meetings on school grounds and stuff."

"She's totally out of her mind," commented Kate.

"A lot of them are falling for her line," said Tara. "I hope Cooper can get more signatures than she does."

"Cooper can pretty much do whatever she wants to," Kate said. "But even if she does, I don't think the school board will change its mind. Cooper said they were dead set against her."

For the rest of the lunch period Kate answered Jessica's and Tara's questions about Wicca. She wasn't always sure that she was doing the best job of

139

it, but being able to talk about what they did in class and what it meant to her made her feel more confident about her ability to explain the Craft to other people. By the time the bell rang she had educated her friends, at least a little bit, and she was feeling better about everything.

Throughout the rest of the day that feeling of confidence grew stronger. As Kate sat in her classes, thinking about how well the conversation with her friends had gone, she started thinking about the next step. Maybe it was time to talk to her parents. The prospect frightened her more than talking to Jessica and Tara had. After all, she had to *live* with her family. But maybe she could do it. If she could explain herself to them the way she'd been able to explain herself to Tara and Jess, maybe they would understand.

She didn't say anything to Annie, Sasha, or Cooper about her decision, partly because she didn't want them to talk it to death but also because she knew it gave her an out if she decided at the last minute not to tell her mother and father. But they were so busy talking about the petition, and about how many people had come up to them during the day to say either positive or negative things, that they didn't notice that she was being more quiet than usual on the walk home.

Mrs. Morgan was in the kitchen when Kate walked into the house. She was experimenting with some new recipes, and they smelled delicious. Kate knew that they would get to enjoy the results of the culinary experiments for dinner, and she was eager to try them.

"What is that?" she asked, sniffing the air.

"Beef stew with rosemary, black mushrooms, and leeks," said her mother. "How does it smell?"

"Great," Kate answered. "What else are you making?"

"Sourdough bread, glazed carrots, and peach cobbler," said her mother.

"What's the occasion?" Kate asked suspiciously. "That's a lot of food even for you."

Mrs. Morgan smiled. "We have a dinner guest coming," she said. "Your Aunt Netty is in town for a few days."

"Aunt Netty," said Kate, suddenly frightened. Her aunt had spent the summer battling cancer. "She's not sick again, is she?"

"No," said her mother. "She's fine. She's just here for a couple of tests to make sure everything is okay. She'll be here around five."

Kate was both happy and apprehensive. She was thrilled that her aunt was coming. But would she still be able to talk to her parents with Aunt Netty around? She wasn't sure.

She went up to her room and pretended to study. But really she was rehearsing in her mind what she was going to say to her parents later. She wanted it to come out just right. If she was overly nervous it was going to come out all wrong, so she tried to relax. But she couldn't keep from looking at the clock every ten minutes, waiting for her aunt to arrive.

Finally she did arrive, opening the front door and calling out, "Hey? Where is everyone?" in a loud, cheerful voice.

Kate raced down the stairs and ran to embrace her aunt.

"Nice hat," Kate said, looking at the Seattle Mariners baseball cap her aunt was wearing.

"Yeah, well, I'm still bald from the chemo," Aunt Netty said.

Kate walked her aunt to the kitchen, where for the next hour they caught up on how she was doing in her battle against cancer and she filled them in on her latest photography assignment, which had been taking pictures of children in a cancer ward.

"The article was my idea," she said. "I think it came out really well. I'll show you some of the shots later. But right now let's eat. If I have to keep smelling that stew I'm going to slobber all over the floor."

Mrs. Morgan started dishing out the stew while Kate set the table and got everything else ready. As they were sitting down Mr. Morgan came in. He was whistling as he walked through the house, which Kate knew meant he was in a good mood. Inwardly she breathed a big sigh of relief. Things were going her way after all.

As they all ate dinner Kate waited for the perfect moment to bring up the issue of Wicca. But in the end she didn't have to do it. Her aunt did it for her.

"Kate, I called Sophia from the bookstore," she said. "Thanks for getting her number for me."

Kate had forgotten all about giving Sophia's phone number to her aunt. She'd asked for it after Sophia and some of the other coven members had performed a healing ritual for her.

"You're not really going to let them do that again, are you?" Mr. Morgan asked, chuckling. "All of that mumbo jumbo?"

"Don't knock it, Joe," Netty said. "I've never felt better."

"It's the *drugs*, Netty," replied Kate's father. "It's medicine. Not some superstitious nonsense." He turned to Kate. "Speaking of which, I see your friend Cooper made it into the paper today."

Kate felt the hopefulness flow out of her. She'd been hoping that her parents hadn't seen the article.

"Cooper?" Mrs. Morgan said. "In the paper?"

Mr. Morgan nodded. "She wants to wear this witch symbol to school," he said. "They're telling her she can't."

"Good," said Mrs. Morgan. "We don't need that kind of stuff in school. Kids are mixed up enough. Did you know about this, Kate?"

"Yeah," Kate said vaguely.

"I told you she and Annie were into something weird," Mrs. Morgan continued. "Witchcraft. Honestly, where are their parents?"

Kate poked at her food, not saying anything.

Suddenly, telling her parents about going to the study group looked like it was definitely out of the picture.

"You know, Teresa, I've been talking to Sophia quite a bit," Aunt Netty said. "I've also been doing a lot of reading. This witchcraft stuff isn't as strange as you think it is."

Mrs. Morgan laughed sharply. "Come on, Netty. I know you've always been into some stuff that was a little out there, but you can't take this seriously. This is just some kid wanting attention."

"How do you know?" Netty countered. "Have you ever read about it? Have you ever tried it?"

"Of course not," Mrs. Morgan said.

"Kate, have these girls tried to get you to do anything?" Mr. Morgan asked suddenly.

"What do you mean, Dad?" Kate said in reply.

"You know, have they tried to get you to do any of this witch stuff?"

Kate swallowed the food in her mouth, barely able to get it down. Once again she was facing a moment of decision. Was she going to tell the truth, or was she going to hide behind half-truths and out-right lies? She'd done that so many times before that she knew it would be easy. All she had to do was tell her father that Annie and Cooper were the ones involved in Wicca and that she didn't have any knowledge of it. He would believe her, dinner would go on as it was, and pretty soon they would all be enjoying peach cobbler and talking about something else. All she had to do was say no.

She looked over at her aunt. Just like her parents, Netty was waiting for Kate to answer, too. But what answer did *she* expect? Had Sophia mentioned to her that Kate was part of the study group? Kate doubted it. Sophia was very insistent upon keeping the identity of the group members private. But Netty was smart, and Kate wouldn't be at all surprised if she had put two and two together and figured out that Kate's friends weren't the only ones with an interest in the Craft.

"No," she said, looking at her father. "They've never asked me to do anything having to do with witchcraft."

Her father nodded, clearly accepting her answer.

Kate took a deep breath. "I'm the one who asked *them* to do it."

CHAPTER 12

"She's not here," Annie said to Cooper.

They'd been standing around the front of Crones' Circle for half an hour, hoping that Kate would appear. She hadn't been in school either, and although they'd tried to call her several times all they'd gotten was the answering machine.

"What do you think happened?" asked Annie worriedly.

Cooper shook her head. "I have no idea," she said. "It's not like Kate to just disappear. Maybe she's sick."

"She seemed fine yesterday," said Annie. "In fact, she seemed to be in a really good mood. Jessica told me today that Kate told her and Tara about being part of the class yesterday."

"She did?" Cooper replied, surprised. "Why didn't she tell us?"

"That's what I'm wondering," said Annie. "I think something is up."

"Well, whatever it is, it will have to wait," said Cooper, looking at her watch. "Class is about to start."

They were heading for the back room when the door to the store opened and someone rushed in. Thinking it was Kate, Cooper and Annie turned. But it wasn't her. It was Netty. When Annie and Cooper saw her they looked at one another in concern. Although Netty knew that they were friends with the owners of the store, she didn't know they were taking a class there.

"Hi," Annie said cautiously as Netty approached them.

"I was hoping you'd be here," said Netty seriously. "We need to talk."

"Why?" Cooper asked. "Did something happen to Kate? Is she okay?"

"She's fine," Netty answered. "Well, she will be. Right now she's really upset."

"About the articles?" said Annie.

Netty shook her head. "No. She told Joe and Teresa about being part of your group."

Cooper's mouth dropped open. "She did not," she said in disbelief.

"She did," Netty replied. "Last night during dinner. They didn't take it well."

"Is that why she wasn't in school today?" Annie asked her.

"They took her to talk to Father Mahoney over at St. Mary's this morning," Netty explained.

"Oh, man," said Cooper. "They tried to deprogram her?"

"Something like that," replied Netty. "They're

really confused and upset. They just don't understand this."

"What exactly did she tell them?" Annie asked.

Netty sighed. "She told them that she had asked the two of you to study witchcraft with her," she said. "Is that true?"

Cooper and Annie looked at one another and shrugged.

"Yes and no," said Annie. "It's more complicated than that."

"Well, she told them it was basically her idea," said Netty. "And she told them about the class and about how she knew who Sophia and the other people were who came and did the ritual for me."

Cooper groaned. "Did she tell them about Tyler?" she asked.

Netty looked confused. "What about Tyler?"

"He's a witch, too," Annie informed her.

Netty smiled. "No," she said. "She didn't bring that up. I think at that point Joe was yelling so much she figured it was best to leave things alone."

"What are they going to do?" asked Cooper.

"I don't honestly know," answered Netty. "They spent most of the night yelling at her. Joe keeps ranting about making her go to St. Basil's instead of Beecher Falls High."

Cooper couldn't help but laugh. "That's where Tyler goes," she said. "She'd probably love it."

"I just came to tell you that you might not see her for a couple of days," Netty said. "They think

I'm out refilling one of my prescriptions, so I should get back. But Kate wanted me to come tell you what happened."

"Can we call her?" Annie asked.

"I wouldn't," Netty answered gently. "You're not exactly on the Morgans' list of favorite people right now."

Annie nodded. "I figured as much," she said. "Would you tell Kate we love her and we're thinking of her?"

Netty smiled. "I'm sure she knows that," she said. "But I'll tell her. And you two say hello to Sophia for me. Tell her I've really enjoyed our talks and I'll call her again soon. Oh, and girls?"

"Yes?" Cooper and Annie said.

"Blessed be," said Netty.

She turned and hurried out of the store, leaving Annie and Cooper to think about what she'd just told them.

"Poor Kate," Annie said. "She finally tells her parents and this is what happens."

"It must be her worst nightmare," added Cooper. "I feel sort of responsible."

"I know," Annie said. "So do I. First Brian and now Kate's parents. Do you think we made a mistake?"

Cooper looked at her for a moment. "No," she said. "I keep telling myself that maybe we did, but I know it's not true."

Annie smiled slightly. "I've been thinking the same thing," she said. "But it still sucks."

"That it does," replied Cooper. "Let's go tell Sophia what happened."

They went into the back and found Sophia. She was talking to Archer, Robin, Julia, and several other people when they approached her. When they explained what had happened to Kate she sighed.

"I'm so sorry to hear that," she said.

"What are we going to do?" Cooper asked.

Sophia shook her head. "Nothing," she said.

"Nothing?" Cooper repeated. "What do you mean?"

"I can't force Kate's parents to let her study Wicca," Sophia told her. "If they tell her she can't come, she can't come. We don't allow minors to take the class if their parents disapprove, no matter how wrong we may think that opinion is."

"But she has to come to class!" said Cooper. "She loves it."

"I know she does," said Sophia gently. "But we can't have her here against the wishes of her parents."

"But can't you at least talk to them?" asked Annie. "You and Netty seem to be friends now. Can't you get her to talk to them?"

Sophia smiled. "I'll see what I can do," she said. "But right now we have a Mabon ritual to do. We'll talk more later."

Since Mabon was one of the minor sabbats, Sophia had decided to make the Mabon ritual open, meaning that people who weren't actually in the class were allowed to attend. She did this from time to time so that class members could invite interested friends who wanted to see what Wicca was all about. As a result there were several people present whom Cooper and Annie didn't recognize. But they weren't thinking a lot about the ritual anyway. Both of them were concerned about Kate and what was going to happen to her.

They stood with the others and listened as the circle was cast. They listened as Sophia explained how Mabon marked the beginning of fall. They watched as two class members, one dressed in a white robe and one in a black robe, carried candles around the circle while singing a song about the light and the dark before meeting in the middle and using their candles to light one single one. Then they joined with the others in doing a spiral dance accompanied by drumming and singing.

When the ritual was over they helped clean up, then joined the others for some refreshments. But neither of them felt much like socializing, and when Cooper said to Annie, "Let's get out of here," she agreed and the two of them slipped out the door.

"Where are we going?" Annie asked as she followed Cooper down the street.

"To Kate's house," answered Cooper.

"We can't!" Annie protested. "Her parents will kill us. And her."

"Her parents aren't going to know," Cooper replied. "Just follow me."

They got on the bus and rode it to their stop.

Getting off, they walked toward the Morgans' house.

"Kate's room is at the back of the house," Cooper told Annie as they walked. "There's a big tree outside her window. We can climb up."

"I don't know," said Annie doubtfully. "What if someone sees us? What if we fall? What if they've locked Kate away in the basement so we can't corrupt her?"

"You are getting *way* too dramatic," Cooper told her. "Stop worrying. You've climbed a tree before, right?"

"When I was like eight or something," said Annie.

"Then you'll be fine," Cooper said.

They reached Kate's house and snuck around the side to the back, avoiding the side they knew the living room was on so Kate's parents couldn't look out and see them. When they were in the backyard they stopped beneath the tree and looked up at Kate's window.

"The light is on," said Cooper. "Now all we have to do is get up there."

Annie looked up at the tree. "It's pretty high," she said doubtfully.

"Just follow me," Cooper answered. She walked to the tree and grabbed the lowest branch, pulling herself up so that she was sitting on it.

"Come on," she said, leaning down and offering Annie her hand. "It's easy."

Annie grabbed Cooper's outstretched fingers.

Putting her feet against the trunk of the tree, she scrambled up beside her friend.

"Not bad, right?" asked Cooper.

"Yeah, but we're only on the first branch," Annie replied.

Cooper stood up and reached for the next branch. The branches of the tree were fairly close together, and it was almost like climbing a ladder. As she climbed Annie followed, trying to do exactly what Cooper was doing. A few minutes later the two of them were sitting on a large branch that extended to Kate's window.

"Now what?" Annie whispered, holding on to the tree for dear life.

"Hang on a second," Cooper said. "I'd only gotten as far as the climbing-the-tree part."

"Now you tell me," said Annie, trying not to look down. She was glad it was dark so she couldn't actually see the ground, which seemed to be thousands of feet below them.

"Kate," Cooper whispered, her voice barely audible.

She paused. There was no answer. "Kate," she called again, a little more loudly.

"She's not going to hear you," Annie said knowingly. "Her window isn't open."

"Do you have a better idea?" Cooper asked testily.

"Why don't you crawl over there and knock?" suggested Annie.

Cooper looked at the window. "What if someone is in there?" she asked.

"Oh, like the whispering thing was so secretive?" Annie countered.

"Good point," said Cooper. She turned and started inching her way along the branch. She went slowly, and Annie kept waiting to hear the branch crack under her weight, but finally she reached the window and knocked gently.

A moment later Kate's face appeared. "What are you guys doing?" she asked.

"Just dropping in," Cooper said.

"Get in here," Kate ordered.

Cooper climbed in the window and motioned for Annie to follow. Still hanging on in fear, she pulled herself along the branch until she felt Cooper and Kate grab her arms and drag her over the windowsill.

"I can't believe you guys did that," Kate said, shutting the window. "If you'd fallen you would have ended up right in the herb garden."

"We thought it would be better than ringing the front doorbell," Cooper told her. "How are you?"

"Not so good," Kate answered. "It's been a rough day. How did you guys know anyway?"

"Netty came to the store and told us," said Annie. "She said your parents went postal."

"That's an understatement," Kate said, sitting down on her bed. "I feel like I'm under house arrest. No phone. No visitors. Nothing."

"Until when?" asked Cooper.

"Until I agree not to see the two of you, or try to go to class, or ever read, see, listen to, or think about anything having to do with witchcraft," Kate said. "I think that just about covers it. Oh, and there's talk of therapy."

Cooper sat down next to Kate. "That is rough," she said.

"I'm really sorry," Annie told her. "I feel like we dragged you into this."

Kate shook her head. "It was my decision," she said. "I needed to do it eventually, and I don't think the reaction would have been any different if I'd waited. I'm just glad Aunt Netty is here. She can at least calm them down a little."

"What about school?" asked Cooper. "They can't just keep you up here forever."

"I'll be back tomorrow," Kate said. "Probably with an armed escort, if my dad has his way, but I'll be back. What did I miss in class tonight?"

"The Mabon ritual," Cooper told her. "It was no big deal. There were a lot of guests. We kind of snuck out right after so we could come here."

Kate sighed. "At least now I guess I can be on the basketball team," she said. "I won't have class to go to."

"You're really going to quit?" Annie asked.

"I don't really have a choice," Kate answered. "I can't sneak out every Tuesday. They'll know where I'm going."

"Does this mean you're giving up on Wicca

altogether?" said Cooper.

"No," Kate said. "I'm not giving up on it. That's something I realized today while everyone was yelling at me. I may have to practice in secret, and wait until I'm out of the house before I do anything in the open, but I'm still going to do it. I haven't come this far to give up now."

"This really sucks," Annie said glumly. "I can't imagine class without you."

"Will they at least let you hang around with us?" Cooper inquired.

"Not any time soon," Kate said. "I told them that I was the one who started all of this, but I don't think they believed me. My father kept asking me why I was covering for you guys. I felt like an international terrorist or something. But they can't keep me from seeing you at school. It's just the other stuff."

"What about Tyler?" Cooper asked. "Have you talked to him?"

"I haven't had a chance," said Kate. "My phone usage is strictly monitored. I'd appreciate it if one of you could call and let him know what happened."

"Sure," Annie said. "I can do that."

Kate smiled sadly. "It's kind of ironic that he and I sort of broke up because I wouldn't tell my parents about being into Wicca and now that I have told them they won't let me see him anyway." Kate sighed. "How were things at school today, anyway?"

"Okay," answered Cooper. "A lot of people have

signed my petition, and a lot have told me how cool they think I am for doing this."

"Same here," said Annie.

"But Sherrie's been doing quite a hatchet job on us—and on Wicca—and she's got a lot of people scared," Cooper said.

"There were also some letters to the editor in today's *Tribune*," said Annie.

"Some people apparently think I'm trying to completely destroy the moral fabric of public education," explained Cooper.

"I guess things really haven't changed all that much since the Middle Ages," Kate said. "You say 'witchcraft' and everybody starts to panic."

"Brian sure did," Annie agreed.

"While Father Mahoney was asking me what kinds of things I'd been doing I kept thinking about all the people who were questioned by the Inquisition," Kate said. "It must have been awful. And Father Mahoney is *nice*. I can't imagine what it would be like being questioned by someone who wanted me dead."

"Probably pretty much like being in Greeley's class," Cooper commented.

"Yeah, what's with her?" Kate said.

Cooper shook her head. "I think she just wants to embarrass me. But we'll show her—right, counselor?"

Annie rolled her eyes. "Don't remind me," she said. "I have to prepare your defense."

"Prepare mine while you're at it." Kate told her.

There was a knock at the door, and a voice said, "Kate?"

"That's my mom," Kate whispered. "You guys have to get out of here."

Annie and Cooper started for the window, but Kate stopped them. "There's not enough time," she said. "Get in the closet."

They ran to the closet and snuck inside, closing the door behind them as Kate walked to her door and opened it.

"Hi," she said. "I was just napping."

Mrs. Morgan walked into the room. "I was just wondering if you wanted some ice cream," she said. "We were about to have some."

"No, thanks," Kate said. "I think I'm just going to go to bed."

"Okay," replied her mother, then added. "Kate, you know your father and I just want what's best for you. We love you."

"I love you, too," Kate answered.

There was a pause as Mrs. Morgan left and Kate shut her door. Then she opened the closet and let Annie and Cooper out.

"You'd better go," she said, sounding tired and unhappy. "I'll see you guys in school tomorrow."

They went to the window and opened it. Cooper turned to Annie. "I'll go first," she said. "That way if you fall into the basil I still have a chance at a clean getaway."

CHAPTER 13

"I can't believe that woman!"

Cooper stormed up to Annie, Kate, and Sasha, who were all gathered around Kate's locker. Cooper thrust the newspaper in her hand at them and shook it.

"Just look at this!" she said.

Her friends scanned the page she was showing them.

"Oh, good Goddess," Sasha said after a minute.

"She didn't," Annie said.

"She did," Kate replied.

Cooper read the article out loud.

'On Monday I wrote an article about Cooper Rivers, a junior at Beecher Falls High School who is fighting for the right to wear a necklace featuring a pentagram, or five-pointed star, after having been ordered by first the principal of the school and then the school board to stop wearing it after several other students and concerned citizens complained. Miss Rivers claims to be a follower of Wicca, or witchcraft, and she says that the necklace is a symbol of her faith.

'Last evening I attended a meeting of the Wicca study group of which Miss Rivers is a part. The meeting was held at Crones' Circle, an esoteric bookstore located in the waterfront area. The occasion was the pagan festival of Mabon, an ancient harvest festival that makes up part of what witches refer to as the Wheel of the Year. The event featured black-robed participants, chanting, and a frenzied dance called by some a "spiral dance."'

"There was *one* person in a black robe!" Annie said. "She was representing the dark half of the year!"

"And what does she mean by 'frenzied'?" Sasha said. "She probably just couldn't keep up."

Cooper continued to read. 'Although nothing overly unusual occurred at this so-called sabbat celebration, I spoke to several noted experts in the occult to ask their opinions about the effects such events might have on impressionable young people. Dr. Margaret Peringer, a psychologist teaching at the University of Oregon and an expert in the field of cults, says, "Young people often can't distinguish between fantasy and reality. This kind of occult game can be very confusing to them, especially if they're suffering from problems such as low self-esteem or feelings of inadequacy. They begin to think that what is essentially role playing is real, and it affects the way they look at the larger world."'

"Now Wicca is a cult?" Kate asked. "I hope my

parents don't read this or I'll be at the therapist in no time."

"It gets worse," Cooper said. "Listen to this. 'Peringer's sentiments are echoed by Leo Brim, founder of Concerned Parents for Children's Safety, a watchdog group that monitors television, film, and print for what it considers dangerous depictions of the occult and other potentially harmful topics. "The idea that witchcraft is something glamorous and fun is increasingly popular," says Brim. "We have television shows featuring teenage witches. There are movies in which young people use magic and sorcery to achieve their ends. And this whole Harry Potter craze has even the smallest kids wanting to be witches and warlocks. If we aren't careful we're going to have a whole nation of children who are swept up in the deadly lies perpetuated by these people."'"

"There's no such thing as warlocks," Sasha said, snorting. "Shows how much he knows.'

"That's not the point," said Annie. "Most people don't know the first thing about what Wicca really is. They'll read this and think this guy knows what he's talking about."

"How did she get all this information about the ritual last night?" Cooper said. "I didn't see her there."

"There were a lot of guests," Annie replied. "She could have worn a wig and we would never have even noticed her. She might not even have really been there. Knowing her, she paid someone to come spy on us."

"I should have known better than to have trusted her," Cooper said angrily. "She used me again. She didn't care about me; she just wanted to do a sensational story. What was I thinking?"

"Did you read this whole thing?" asked Annie, who had taken the paper from Cooper and was perusing it.

"No," Cooper said. "Just the first page. What else is there?"

'While Cooper Rivers does have some supporters in her crusade to carry the banner of witchcraft in public schools, many more people seem to be opposed to letting her wear a symbol some believe to be offensive and potentially threatening to the safety of other students,' Annie read.

'Sherrie Adams, a classmate of Ms. Rivers, has organized a petition to keep the ban on pentagrams and other occult-related symbols. "I don't think she should be able to wear something like that," Miss Adams says. "I, for one, find it very unnerving to see someone wearing a symbol associated with Satanism. I know a lot of other people feel the same way I do but they're afraid to say anything because they think Cooper and her friends might put a curse on them."

'Ms. Adams says that while she does fear retaliation for her actions, she is committed to having the concerns of herself and other students opposed to overturning the school board decision heard. She has so far collected almost 100 signatures in support of the ban, and she hopes to have many times that number before September 30, the date on which the board will hear arguments from both sides in this matter.'

"Oh, now *both* sides are going to get to speak at the meeting?" said Cooper. "I don't suppose this has anything to do with the fact that Sherrie just happens to be the daughter of one of the members. I see Amanda just happened to leave out that little piece of information."

"She did," Annie confirmed. "But she made sure she pointed out that you 'live in historic Welton House with her mother, Janet Rivers, a third grade school teacher at Beecher Falls Elementary School, and her father, Stephen Rivers, a successful attorney.'"

"We're doomed," Cooper said, slumping against the lockers. "Everyone is going to read this and believe what she wrote. They're all going to think we're killing babies or cutting the heads off goats or something."

"Where did she find those 'experts' anyway?" Kate asked.

"She probably called up Dr. Laura and asked her for recommendations," Cooper answered.

"And do you think Sherrie really has a hundred signatures?" asked Sasha.

"I have around sixty," Cooper said. "If she has more than I do I'd be really surprised. I think she just made that up to make it look like people are supporting her."

"Still," Annie said. "I think we'd better double our efforts today."

"Hey, Rivers." The girls looked up to see John Reynolds looking at them. He was holding a copy of the *Tribune* and grinning. "I hope you have your free speech arguments all lined up. It looks like I just got myself some pretty heavy artillery."

"I don't know," Cooper shot back. "From what I hear, your artillery isn't all that impressive, Reynolds."

John turned and walked away while Cooper's friends laughed.

"He's right, though," Annie said a moment later. "We have to come up with something good if we want to win that debate in class."

"It's not a debate," Cooper said. "It's a setup. Greeley wants us to look like fools."

"Then we have to find a way to not look like fools," Annie replied.

"If it isn't the Beecher Falls coven," said T.J., appearing from between the rows of lockers. "What are you witchlets up to this time?"

"We're not a coven," Cooper told him.

"I know. I know," her boyfriend said. "But see how up on the lingo I am?"

"Very nice," Kate said, congratulating him.

"So what *are* you guys up to?" T.J. asked. "You look grim."

Annie handed him the newspaper. "Read," she said.

T.J. read the piece. As he did the look on his face changed from one of happiness to one of surprise to one of anger.

"This is that same woman who wrote the piece about you and the dead girl, right?" he said.

"That would be her," said Cooper.

T.J. frowned. "I'd like to get her alone for about ten minutes," he said. "Someone needs to kick her butt and good."

"I get first dibs," Cooper told him.

"Where does she get off?" asked T.J. sounding angrier than any of them had ever heard him sound.

"It doesn't do any good to be mad at Amanda Barclay," Annie told him. "Trust me. We've been there. What we need to do now is concentrate on getting enough signatures on our petition so that Sherrie's looks like a laundry list in comparison."

"What's the plan, then?" T.J. asked.

"To the library," Annie said. "Follow me."

They all trooped down the hallway to the library. Inside, Annie turned to Cooper. "The petition, please."

Cooper opened her backpack and pulled out the petition. Annie took it from her and walked to the copy machine. She fished in her jeans pocket for change and plunked it into the machine. A few moments later she handed each of her friends a copy of the petition.

"If we can each get twenty more signatures, added to the sixty or so Cooper already has, we'll have more than enough," she said. "That's our goal. So get to work, people."

"Yes, Sarge!" T.J. said, making them all laugh.

They left the library and went to their first period classes. Although they saw one another in the halls and checked in whenever they had classes together, they mostly weren't in the same place until fifth period, when they all congregated in the cafeteria. Cooper, Sasha, Annie, and T.J. had to skip their fifth period classes to do it, but it had been determined that a midday strategy session was in order.

"I got ten," Sasha said, putting her petition on the table in front of Annie, who was doing the adding up.

"Add twelve for me," T.J. said. "I got all the guys in shop to sign it."

"I have fourteen," said Kate proudly. "Including two teachers—Mr. Niemark and Mrs. Hannity."

"The home ec teacher?" Cooper said. "How'd that happen?"

"She liked the way I made a soufflé last year," said Kate. "You'd be surprised. She's pretty hip for an old lady."

"That's thirty-six," Annie said, scribbling in the margins of her notebook. "Plus the eleven I got and however many you got, Cooper."

"Make that seventeen more," Cooper said.

"Where'd you find seventeen people?" Kate asked, amazed.

Cooper grinned. "You know all those kids who

spend their breaks smoking behind the building?" she said. "The ones everyone is afraid of? We go *way* back."

"Let's hear it for the ravers," Annie said as she totaled up the figures. "That gives us sixty-four new votes which, added to the fifty-seven Cooper already had, gives us one hundred and twenty-one. Not bad."

"Not bad?" Cooper said. "That's like a fifth of the school or something."

"But we still need twenty-nine more to make a hundred and fifty," Annie reminded her.

"What are you guys doing?" asked Tara, coming up and sitting beside Annie as Jessica sat beside Cooper. "Shouldn't you be in class?"

"We're trying to beat Sherrie at the petition game," Kate explained.

"Can we help?" Jessica asked.

"Want to collect some signatures for us?" Annie asked.

"Why not?" replied Tara.

"Here you go, then," Annie said, handing them blank petitions. "I made some extras."

"I'll be right back," Jessica said, getting up.

"Me, too," added Tara.

"Where are they going?" T.J. asked as the two girls went in different directions.

"I don't know," Kate said. "We'll have to wait and find out."

Ten minutes later Jessica and Tara came back to the table and handed Annie their sheets.

"You've got fifteen signatures!" Annie said to Tara.

Tara nodded. "Those are all the cheerleaders Sherrie cheesed off when she tried to pull that stunt to become head of the varsity squad," she said. "They were more than happy to sign."

"Did they know what it was?" asked Kate.

"Probably not," Tara said. "They just knew Sherrie was against it, and that was enough for most of them."

"And you got thirteen," Annie said, looking at Jessica's sheet. "How'd you do that so quickly?"

"Easy," Jessica replied. "Three from the string quartet I play in, seven from the violin section, two more clarinetists, and one from the guy who plays the timpani and has a little crush on me."

"That's a grand total of one hundred and forty-nine," said Annie.

"We need one more," said Cooper. "One more lousy signature. Who can we get?"

"Bailey Maron," Kate said.

"Who?" asked Sasha.

"Bailey Maron," Kate repeated. "She's sitting right over there."

"Who's Bailey Maron?" asked Jessica.

"She was Elizabeth Sanger's best friend," Annie answered. "You remember. The dead girl whose murderer Cooper helped the police catch."

"I'll be right back," said Cooper.

She took one of the petitions and walked over

to where Bailey Maron was eating lunch with some of her friends. The others watched as Cooper sat down and started talking to Bailey. The younger girl nodded her head a few times, then took the pen Cooper handed her and signed. Cooper said something that made Bailey laugh, and then Cooper stood up and walked back to the table.

"There you go," she said, handing the petition to Annie. "Number one-fifty. Let's hear it for ghost power."

"I want to count them again just to make sure," said Annie, methodically going through the lists. The others watched as she ran her pencil down the rows, her mouth moving silently as she counted.

"Yep," she said when she was done. "We have one hundred and fifty."

"They *have* to take this seriously now," Cooper said. "There's no way Sherrie has that many signatures. No way." She looked around at all of her friends. "And I could never have done it without you guys. Thanks."

"It's still not over," Annie said. "This is just the first step."

"Leave it to you to point out the downside," Cooper said.

"Forgive me," Annie said. "I was recently dumped. I'm slightly bitter."

"Well, cheer up," said Cooper, rubbing her head. "It's not like me to be optimistic, but I feel really good about this."

CHAPTER 14

"That was just what I needed," Cooper said as she walked out of the theater with Sasha, Annie, T.J., and Tyler on Friday night.

It had been Tyler's idea to go to the movie. Annie had called him on Wednesday night to tell him about Kate, and he had suggested they all get together on Friday evening to try to have at least a little bit of a break from everything that was going on. Cooper had suspected that he also wanted to talk about Kate with people who knew her.

She'd been right. Tyler had talked about Kate almost constantly since they met at the theater. He'd stopped when the movie started, but now that they were outside he started up again almost immediately.

"You're sure Kate's okay?" he asked anxiously.

"She's fine," Cooper said, even though she knew it wasn't true. Kate was a mess. Her parents were still being really rough on her, and she'd cried for half an hour in the girls' bathroom at school that afternoon when she was supposed to be in Ms. Ableman's science class.

"This is all my fault," said Tyler. "I should never have insisted that she tell her parents."

"It wasn't just you," said Annie. "Cooper and I were pressuring her, too."

"I know," Tyler replied. "But I feel like I pushed her away when she needed me to stick by her."

"She still needs you," said Cooper. "Now more than ever."

"And just how am I supposed to do that?" Tyler asked. "I can't see her. I can't even call her."

"Why not E-mail her?" T.J. said.

"Unless her parents are reading her E-mail, too," Annie pointed out.

"It's worth trying," said Tyler. "I can't get to her any other way except through you guys, and that's just not the same."

"I'll write her address down for you," said Cooper. "You can try it when you get home."

"Sasha, that was a really cool letter that Thea wrote to the paper," T.J. said as they continued to walk down the street.

"Thea wrote a letter?" Tyler asked.

"Yeah," Sasha answered. "To the *Tribune*, in response to Amanda Barclay's article. She talked about how she's a witch and how she's raising a teenager who is also into the Craft and how it has nothing to do with Satan worship or anything stupid like that. It was really a great letter."

"It was certainly a lot better than the other seven they ran that all supported the ban on occult symbols in schools," Annie remarked. "Some of those letters were really hostile."

"My favorite was the one from the guy who said that if teenagers are allowed to learn about witchcraft they'll get pregnant and do drugs," said Cooper. "Where did *that* come from?"

"I just wish more people had written letters like Thea's," said Annie.

"I know," Sasha agreed. "I have the coolest mom in the world."

Cooper noticed Sasha's use of the word *mom* in reference to Thea. She had never called her that before, and it made Cooper happy to hear it. It meant that Sasha really was thinking of Beecher Falls as her permanent home, and of Thea as her permanent family. *At least one thing is going well*, she thought.

They were almost to the bus stop when Cooper noticed the three guys watching them from across the street. They were standing in front of the Bull Pen, a sports bar popular with the jock crowd from nearby Jasper College. One was wearing a baseball cap, one had on a Jasper Bulldogs sweatshirt, and one of them was holding a big plastic cup in his hand.

"Hey," the guy in the baseball cap called out. "Aren't you that witch?"

"Just ignore him," Annie said to Cooper.

The guy jogged across the road and stopped in

front of the group. "Hey," he said again. "I recognize your picture from the paper. You're that witch girl, right?"

"Yeah," Cooper said. "I am."

The guy laughed and waved to his friends. "Hey, guys, I told you it was her."

His friends crossed the street, too, and the three of them stood looking at Cooper and the others with grins on their faces.

"Is that the necklace?" the one holding the cup asked, nodding at the pentacle visible around Cooper's neck.

Cooper nodded. She wondered what the three boys wanted. They seemed friendly enough, but something troubled her about the situation. She wished they would just get out of their way so she and her friends could keep walking.

"Let's see that," said the guy in the sweatshirt. He reached out his hand and lifted the pentacle.

"Hey!" Cooper said, swatting at his hand. "Do you mind?"

The guy pulled his hand away and glared at her. "I just wanted to see the thing," he said. "Cool it."

"Better watch out, Doug," the guy with the cup told his buddy. "She might zap you or something."

The three guys laughed, but Doug didn't try to touch Cooper's necklace again.

"Let's go," said T.J., starting to walk by the college guys.

"Wait, wait, wait," said the one in the cap, putting his hand on T.J.'s chest. "We're not done talking to witchgirl here."

He pushed T.J. away and stood in front of Cooper. "So what kind of powers do you have?" he asked. "Can you make me fall in love with you?"

Cooper knew she should play it cool, but the guy's attitude was really bugging her. "Why?" she asked. "Can't you get a girl on your own?"

His friends hooted. "She told you, Wayne," Doug said.

Wayne sneered at Cooper. "Who the hell do you think you are?" he asked her. "Some high school punk who thinks she's hot stuff because she wears a stupid necklace?"

"And who the hell do you think *you* are?" Sasha asked, coming to stand beside Cooper. "Some college punk who thinks he's hot stuff because he wears a stupid baseball cap?"

Wayne looked at her, then turned to his friends. "Get a load of this one," he said, snickering.

The guy holding the cup approached Sasha. "I suppose you're a witch, too?" he asked.

"Maybe I am," Sasha said.

"Maybe you should give her the test, Todd," Wayne told his friend. "What did they use to do to witches, burn them? Maybe you should see if she burns."

"Maybe you should shut your mouth."

Cooper turned and looked at Tyler, who had just spoken. He was glaring at the three college guys with an expression of pure anger on his face. Cooper could see he was shaking, and she knew he must be both frightened and furious.

"Who's that?" Todd asked. "Your boyfriend?"

"No, I'm her boyfriend," T.J. answered, moving closer to Todd.

Todd took a lighter out of his pocket and flicked it on. He moved the flame closer to Sasha's face. "What do you think?" he said tauntingly. "Think you'll burn?"

Sasha looked at him coldly. The next thing Cooper heard was a splash as the cup fell from his hand and its contents went everywhere. Then Todd was on the ground, holding his crotch and moaning loudly. The lighter clattered to the sidewalk beside him and sputtered out in a puddle of beer.

"She kicked me," he gasped as his friends looked on in astonishment.

Wayne and Doug looked at Todd on the ground. Then they looked at Cooper and the others, their faces contorted in anger. Suddenly, Wayne leaped forward, trying to grab Sasha. But T.J. jumped between them and grabbed Wayne by the shirt, swinging him sideways.

Doug came at Cooper, bellowing, "You stupid witch." She put her arms up to ward him off but not before he'd grabbed her by the throat and started to choke her. She felt his fingers pressing against her windpipe, cutting off the air. She tried to knee him, like Sasha had Todd, but she was thrown off balance and could only grab at his face, trying to push him away.

Everything seemed to move too quickly. She couldn't get her bearings and she couldn't think. Out of the corner of her eye she saw T.J. and Wayne swinging at each other. She also saw Todd rising to his knees behind Sasha, who wasn't looking in his direction. She wanted to call out and warn her, but she couldn't.

Then Doug was pulled backward and his grip on Cooper's throat loosened. Cooper heard someone screaming and then looked up to see Annie hanging off Doug's back. She was pounding his head with her free hand and yelling at him to leave them all alone. If she hadn't been trying to gasp in air, Cooper would have laughed at the sight of the big college jock turning around and around as he tried to knock little Annie off.

Todd was almost standing again, and Cooper could see that his goal was to get to Sasha. "Behind you!" she called out just as Todd lurched forward.

Sasha turned and punched Todd square in the stomach. He doubled forward, clutching his gut, and she nailed him again in the face. Blood flew from his nose as he staggered back, crying out in pain before turning and running off into the darkness.

That took care of one guy, but there were still two left. Cooper looked at Doug and saw that Tyler had come to Annie's aid. But T.J. was still fighting

Wayne all by himself. Both of them had blood on their faces, and they were screaming and swearing at one another as they continued to fight. Cooper knew that T.J.'s older brothers had taught him a thing or two about boxing, and even though he was smaller than the college guy he was holding his own. While this encouraged her, she also knew that it would enrage Wayne, who probably wasn't too happy about having his butt kicked by a high school kid.

Before anyone could do anything else the sound of sirens filled the air and Cooper saw the flashing lights that signaled the arrival of a police car. Hearing it, Wayne and Doug took off, running after their already departed friend. Cooper ran over to T.J. and put her arm around him.

"Are you okay?" she asked.

T.J. wiped some blood from his lip, which had been split open. "Yeah," he said. "I'm fine."

"That eye is going to swell shut," said Cooper, touching the puffy and already bruising skin over T.J.'s right eye.

The police car came to a stop and two officers jumped out.

"What's going on?" asked one of the officers, a young woman with the name Watson on her tag.

"Those guys attacked us," Annie told them.

"Do you know why?" asked the second officer, an older man whose name tag read Meers.

"Because of me," Cooper informed them.

The officers looked at her closely. "You're the girl from the paper," said Officer Watson.

"That's why they attacked us," said Cooper. "They saw my picture. They were harassing me and my friends, and when we told them to knock it off they came at us."

Officer Meers shook his head. "Is everyone all right?" he asked.

"A little bloody, but okay," T.J. told him. "I think they got the worst of it, to tell you the truth. After all, there are five of us and only three of them."

Officer Watson sniffed the air. "Were you drinking tonight?" she asked.

"That was their beer," Sasha said. "That guy dropped it when I nailed him in the jewels. That's his lighter, too."

The officer looked at her inquisitively. "Excuse me?" she said.

"Sorry," Sasha said. "When I kicked him in the . . . you know."

The officer nodded, smiling slightly. "I see," she said, bending down to pick up the lighter. "I'll just take this as evidence in case we need it later."

"Where did you learn to fight like that anyway?" Annie asked her. "You went all *Charlie's Angels* on that guy."

"Live on the streets for a while," Sasha told her. "You learn some stuff."

"You weren't so bad yourself," said Cooper to Annie.

"Please," Annie said. "All I did was hang on for dear life."

"You all seem to be okay," Officer Meers said. "At least for the most part," he added as he examined T.J.'s battered face. "Why don't you let us drive you home? It's probably safer than walking. Those guys might still be hanging around."

Cooper hated the idea of needing a police escort home, but she agreed. The five of them managed to squeeze into the back of the patrol car, and they left. As they drove, Officer Watson asked them what they could tell her about the guys who had attacked them. Cooper told them their names and described what they were wearing.

"They shouldn't be too hard to find if they go to Jasper," Officer Meers remarked. "We'll drive over there after we drop you off and see what we can find."

They dropped T.J. off first. Officer Meers walked him to his front door, and Cooper saw the policeman talking to Mr. McAllister when he came to see why his son was being brought home by a cop. When they were done T.J. turned and waved to Cooper as he went inside.

Annie was next, and then Cooper, as Sasha and Tyler were in the opposite direction. As Cooper got out of the car she looked at her friends and said, "Sorry about this, you guys."

"It's okay," said Tyler.

"Yeah," Sasha added. "No problem."

"I'll see you tomorrow," Cooper told Sasha. "And I'll talk to you later," she said to Tyler as she shut the door.

Officer Watson walked her to the door. Before Cooper could even get her key out of her pocket the door swung open and her mother rushed out.

"What happened?" she said. "Is anyone dead?"

"No, Mrs. Rivers," the officer said. "Your daughter was attacked by some college boys."

"Oh, my God!" said Cooper's mother, grabbing her and hugging her tightly. "Are you okay?"

"Except that now I can't breathe, yeah," said Cooper.

Her mother released her and looked at her face. "What happened to your neck?" she asked.

"One of them tried to choke me," said Cooper. "He was trying to rip my pentacle off."

"That damn necklace again!" Mrs. Rivers said angrily, surprising both Cooper and Officer Watson.

"Can we talk about this inside?" asked Cooper, nodding toward the police officer.

"Your daughter and her friends handled themselves very well, Mrs. Rivers," said Officer Watson. "You should be proud of her. Cooper, I may need to talk to you again if we find those guys."

"Okay," Cooper said. "And thanks."

The officer left, and Cooper followed her mother into the house. Her father, hearing the conversation, had come down from his upstairs office.

"What happened?" he asked.

"Cooper was almost killed," said Mrs. Rivers.

"I wasn't almost killed," Cooper protested. "Some guys got in my face because of the newspaper article."

Mr. Cooper sighed. "I have half a mind to file a lawsuit against Amanda Barclay," he said.

"Why?" Mrs. Rivers snapped. "You and Cooper are the ones who talked to her in the first place. She's just doing her job."

Cooper turned to her mother. "Are you blaming me for this?" she asked.

"If you didn't insist on wearing that, and talking about it every chance you get, then this kind of thing wouldn't happen," Mrs. Rivers answered.

"So you'd rather I just let people walk all over my rights?" Cooper said.

"I don't think we should talk about this right now," Mr. Rivers said calmly. "Everyone is upset."

"I wasn't upset until a second ago," Cooper said. "Are you saying you think the school board is right, Mom?"

"I've told you before what I think," answered Mrs. Rivers.

"So what you're saying is you don't support me in this," Cooper said.

"Cooper—" her father said.

"I'm just trying to clarify things, Dad," said Cooper.

Mrs. Rivers looked at her daughter. "No," she

said evenly. "I don't support you."

"Janet," Mr. Rivers said. "Cooper was just attacked."

"She asked me, Stephen," said Cooper's mother. "She asked me what I think. And what I think is that you and she are doing something very foolish. Look what kind of trouble it's already caused. Cooper could have been killed."

"But I wasn't," Cooper protested.

"But you could have been," said Mrs. Rivers. "Easily. And this isn't the first time. If your friends hadn't been there, and if the police hadn't come, we might be visiting you in a morgue right now. You might think that necklace is worth dying for, but I'm sorry, I don't."

Cooper turned away. "I'm going to bed," she said.

She ran upstairs. She knew that she should stay and talk the matter out with her parents. That would be the mature thing to do. But she was tired and angry. She was angry at the three guys who had attacked her. She was angry at Amanda Barclay for writing such a biased article about her. And she was angry at her mother for being unsupportive.

But mostly she was angry because what she feared the most was that her mother might be right.

CHAPTER 15

Kate clicked on the mail icon on her computer screen. It was Saturday morning. She'd been on-line, looking up information for an English assignment, when suddenly the little flag on the mailbox had gone up and the annoying chime indicating that she'd received an E-mail had sounded.

It's probably just more junk mail, she thought as she opened her mail to see what it was. She'd only had her E-mail account for a little while, and she hadn't given the address to very many people. So far the only E-mails she'd gotten had been from Cooper and Annie.

But when she saw the subject line her spirits immediately lifted. "Merry Meet!" it said. Seeing the familiar Wiccan greeting was like hearing from an old friend. But who had sent her such a thing? She checked the screen name. "RowanTree," she said out loud. "Who could that be?"

Then it hit her—Rowan was Tyler's mother's name. But why would Rowan be E-mailing her? And how would she have gotten Kate's E-mail address anyway?

She clicked on the E-mail and watched it open. Then she began reading.

Dear Kate:

It's me, Tyler—not my mom. I was afraid you'd delete the message if you saw it was from me. I had to write you—Cooper and Annie told me what happened with your parents. I can't tell you how sorry I am, Kate. I guess having a mother who is into Wicca made me think that other parents would understand, too. I guess I should have known after what happened with my dad, but I really wanted things to be different for you.

I wish there was something I could do to help. I feel like this is all my fault. If I hadn't pressured you then you could have told your parents in your own time.

I don't really know what else to say. It's kind of weird writing all this on a computer screen instead of saying it to your face. So I guess for now I'll just say that I love you and I'm thinking about you. I hope everything works out. I really do.

Love,
Tyler

Kate printed out Tyler's E-mail and read it again. Reading Tyler's words, she felt like crying. She missed him so much. But he was wrong. Nothing that had happened was his fault. Yes, he'd told her that she should tell her parents about studying witchcraft. But she'd known for a long time that she would have to tell them eventually. She couldn't let Tyler think that he was responsible for her situation.

She hit the reply button and began to type a response to Tyler.

Dear Tyler:

I'm so glad that you wrote. Yes, things have been a little rough. But I don't want you to think that any of it is because of you. You're the best thing that has ever happened to me. It's not your fault that my parents don't understand what Wicca is and why it's important to me. That's their problem.

I don't know what's going to happen. But whatever it is, I want you to know that I

"Kate? Are you ready to go?"

Kate jumped, startled by her mother's appearance in the doorway. In her nervousness, she accidentally dropped the printout of Tyler's E-mail on the floor. Her mother bent down and picked it up.

"Here you are," she said, starting to hand it back. Then she looked at it more closely and retracted her hand. She read the printout as Kate watched her face.

"What is this?" Mrs. Morgan asked.

"Just an E-mail," said Kate, knowing there was no point in trying to lie. It was pretty obvious what it was her mother had in her hands.

Mrs. Morgan walked over and snapped the computer's off switch. The screen blanked out and the room filled with the sound of the motor winding down. *I didn't get to send my reply,* Kate thought as she stared at the black screen.

"I thought we told you—no contact with those people," her mother said.

"But it's Tyler," protested Kate.

"I see that," said her mother. "So he's involved with them, too, is he? I suppose I should have known. Your father never did like him. And there I was, defending him and saying he was a nice boy."

"He *is* nice!" Kate yelled.

"Don't speak to me that way," snapped her mother.

"Why?" Kate said. "Because you're too narrow-minded to listen to what anybody else thinks?"

Her mother glared at her. Kate glared back. She'd never spoken so harshly to her mother before. In fact, they rarely fought about anything. But things had changed. Over the past few days her mother had turned into someone Kate didn't recognize. While she was sure her mother felt the same way about her, that didn't stop her from being angry.

"What's going on?" Kate's father stuck his head inside the door of her room.

"Nothing," Mrs. Morgan told her husband. "Kate and I were just having a discussion."

"Well, let's get going," replied Mr. Morgan. "We're going to be late if we don't hurry."

He left the room, leaving Mrs. Morgan with Kate.

"Thanks," Kate said, knowing that her mother had done her a favor by not telling her father about the E-mail from Tyler.

"Don't thank me," said Mrs. Morgan. "Just get ready."

She left the room, shutting the door behind her. Kate was tempted to turn on the computer and rewrite her E-mail to Tyler, but she knew she'd get in huge trouble if she did. Instead she got up, put on a sweater, and went downstairs.

"We'll be back in a couple of hours," Mrs. Morgan said to Netty as she, Kate, and Mr. Morgan headed out the door.

"Okay," Netty called from her place on the living room couch, where she was sitting and reading a book. "I'll see you later."

Kate caught her aunt's eye as she left the house. *Good luck*, Aunt Netty mouthed silently.

Kate smiled back at her and nodded. She would need some good luck. Her parents were taking her to see a therapist recommended to them by Father Mahoney. Kate had protested, telling her parents that she didn't need to talk to a shrink, but they had insisted.

The whole way there she didn't say a word. Neither did her mother. Mr. Morgan, though, kept up a steady stream of conversation, talking about everything from the weather to the latest sports scores. *He's trying to pretend that everything is fine*, Kate thought as she sat scrunched into the backseat. In a way she felt sorry for her father. He really didn't know the first thing about Wicca, and she was sure he was really confused. *If he'd just listen, maybe I could explain it to him*, she thought. But every time she even tried to bring up the subject he changed it.

Twenty minutes later her father pulled the car into the parking lot of a nondescript office complex. They all got out of the car and walked toward the entrance of one of the buildings. When they arrived, Kate looked at the names on the directory: Dr. Sylvia Hagen, Dr. J. Phillip Olberman, Dr. Carolyn Joyce. *I wonder which one gets to probe my brain*, she thought unhappily.

Her father opened the door and they went inside into what could have been the waiting room for any doctor's or dentist's office. A receptionist sat behind a counter, and there were chairs and a couch arranged around a coffee table littered with magazines.

"Can I help you?" asked the receptionist.

"I'm Joseph Morgan," said Kate's father. "I'm here with my daughter, Kate."

The receptionist looked at a list attached to her clipboard. "Okay," she said. "Could you have Kate fill this out, please?" She handed Mr. Morgan another clipboard with a pen attached to it. "Then Dr. Hagen will see you."

Dr. Hagen, thought Kate. At least now she knew the identity of the person who would be torturing her. She walked over to one of the chairs and sat down as her father handed her the clipboard.

Kate looked at the form. It was a list of questions, all of them apparently pertaining to her mental health. For each one she was supposed to circle yes or no. She read the first question: Have you recently been feeling depressed?

Not until my parents accused me of cavorting with the devil, she thought as she circled no.

She went through the list quickly, mostly circling no for them. *Who makes up this stuff?* she wondered as she looked at question 7. Have you ever felt like there was no point to life? *Only like every other day*, Kate thought, circling no. She wasn't about to give Dr. Hagen anything to work with. She did, however, answer yes to question 13 (Do you ever wish you were someone else?) and 22 (Do you think the idea of therapy is a waste of time?).

"All done," she said, handing the form back to the receptionist.

"Thanks," the woman said. "Have a seat and we'll call you in a minute."

Kate returned to her chair and flopped into it.

Her mother and father sat on the couch, not saying anything. Her father was thumbing through a back issue of *Cosmopolitan*.

"Looking for tips on how to ease the embarrassment of stretch marks?" Kate asked, feeling hostile.

Mr. Morgan tossed the magazine onto the coffee table.

A moment later a woman walked into the waiting room. She was a little shorter than Kate, and very skinny. Her salt-and-pepper-colored hair was cut short, almost in a brush cut gone out of control. It stuck up at odd angles, almost like Cooper's did. She wore glasses, and when she smiled Kate could see that her teeth were a little crooked.

"Kate?" she said.

Kate stood up, as did her parents.

"Hi," said the woman. "I'm Dr. Hagen. Are you ready to come in?"

"I think so," said Mrs. Morgan.

"Oh, not you," said the doctor. "I'll just be talking to Kate today."

Mrs. Morgan looked a little surprised at the doctor's announcement, but she didn't say anything. She sat back down as Dr. Hagen smiled at Kate. "Shall we?"

Kate followed her down a hallway and into an office. The doctor shut the door and indicated a large armchair. "Have a seat," she said.

"No couch?" Kate asked.

The doctor laughed. "Those went out with Freud," she said.

Kate looked around the office. It wasn't at all what she had expected. It was more like sitting in someone's living room than it was being at a shrink's. Then again, she'd never been to a shrink before. The only one she'd ever seen was on television, on *The Sopranos*, and that woman always looked like she had either just peed herself or was about to. Dr. Hagen wasn't like that at all.

"Tell me why you're here," the doctor said straight off.

So much for the small talk, Kate thought as she searched for an answer. *I guess when you pay by the hour every second counts.* "Don't you know?" she said finally, hoping she could find out exactly what her parents had told Dr. Hagen.

"I know your parents are concerned about you," replied the doctor.

Kate snorted. "I'm sure they are," she said. "Concerned parents always assume their children need psychological help."

"You don't think you do?"

"No," Kate said. "I don't. I think I was doing pretty well until they freaked out on me. I was doing okay in school, I had friends I really liked, and everything was cool."

"Why did your parents freak out?" asked the doctor, only when she said "freak out" it sounded normal, not like when most adults said it, trying to sound like they were with it.

Kate looked at her. The doctor was sitting with a pencil in her hands, not writing anything down or anything but just holding it. She looked back at Kate with a totally neutral expression, and Kate had no idea whether she knew about the witch thing or not.

"I told them that I'm interested in Wicca," she said, deciding that being honest would save time.

Dr. Hagen nodded. "And they were upset by this?"

Kate rolled her eyes. "I'm here, aren't I?"

"You're right," said the doctor. "I retract the question. How about *why* do you think they were upset by that?"

Kate sighed. That was the million-dollar question. "They think it's dangerous," she answered. "They think I'm doing something bad, I guess."

"Have they said that?" the doctor asked.

"They said that they don't think it's right to be playing around with things like that," said Kate. "Those were their exact words."

"But they never really said what it was exactly those things are?" Dr. Hagen said.

"No," Kate said. "There was basically just a lot of yelling. And grounding."

Dr. Hagen wrote something in her notebook.

"Let me ask you something," Kate said. "Do you know what Wicca is?"

Dr. Hagen nodded. "In addition to my degree in

psychology, I also hold a master's in comparative religion," she said. "I met Dennis when he was studying at the seminary and I was using their library."

"Dennis?" Kate asked, confused.

"Father Mahoney," Dr. Hagen told her. "We've known each other for more than thirty years."

"That explains why he told my parents to bring me to you," Kate said. "So you studied Wicca?"

Dr. Hagen shook her head. "Not really studied it, no," she said. "But I do know what it is."

"And do *you* think it's dangerous?" Kate asked.

"I'm supposed to ask you the questions," answered the doctor. "Why don't you tell me how you feel about it."

Kate leaned back, relaxing for the first time since she'd entered Dr. Hagen's office. Did the doctor want to know how she *really* felt about Wicca, or did she want to hear something that would make her declare Kate totally fine and send her home with a clean bill of health?

"I think it *can* be dangerous," Kate said, thinking about her first early attempts at casting spells and how badly they'd turned out. "But only when you don't know what you're doing."

"And you know what you're doing?" asked Dr. Hagen.

"I'm getting better at it," Kate said. "I've learned a lot from the study group I'm in. Those people have been practicing a lot longer than I have. That doesn't mean I don't screw up sometimes. I do. But that's sort of how it works, right? You make mistakes and you learn from them."

"That's what we hope," the doctor commented.

Kate and the doctor talked at length about Wicca and Kate's rituals. Kate felt herself relaxing with the low-key therapist. Kate leaned forward in her chair. "Look," she said. "I know my parents brought me here so that you would get me to say that witchcraft is bad and that I won't do it anymore and that I'll be a good girl and go to church and all of that. But I *like* Wicca. I like what it stands for. I like my friends in the Craft and I like who I am when I'm involved in it."

"You didn't like yourself before?" Dr. Hagen said.

Kate sat back. "I thought I did," she said. "But I think what I actually liked was who people thought I was."

"And who is the real you?"

Kate thought about the question. "I guess that's what I'm finding out, isn't it? I mean, do you ever really find out who you are?"

"But you believe that your involvement in Wicca is helping you do that?" the doctor asked, as usual answering Kate's question with another one.

"Yes," Kate said. "I do. I just wish my parents understood that."

A buzzer sounded, making Kate jump. "What was that?"

"The timer," said Dr. Hagen, holding up a plain

old egg timer that had been sitting beside her chair unnoticed by Kate. "It means our time is up, at least for this week."

"You mean I have to come back?" Kate said.

"Only if you want to," the doctor replied. "Do you?"

Kate looked at her. Dr. Hagen had barely said anything during the session, and even then she'd only asked questions. But somehow Kate felt a little better than she had when she'd come in. Finally someone besides her friends was listening to her talk about why it was important for her to be involved in witchcraft. Although she didn't see how this was going to help her with the situation with her parents, it felt good to be able to talk and have someone listen.

"Yes," she said, surprised at her answer. "I'd like to come back."

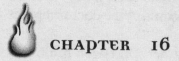

CHAPTER 16

"It was really horrible," Sasha said. "They were all yelling and everything was a mess."

At first Annie thought that Sasha was telling Kate about the incident with the three college guys on Friday night. She had missed the first part of the conversation, walking in as Kate was taking her books from her locker on Monday morning.

"Did you tell her how you kicked that guy?" Annie said.

"You kicked the social worker?" Kate said, clearly shocked.

"Social worker?" repeated Annie. "He was no social worker. He was some jerky frat boy."

"Wrong story," Sasha said. "I was filling Kate in on what went down over the weekend."

"You mean there was *more*?" said Annie. It was her turn to sound shocked.

"What do you mean, more?" Kate asked Annie. "Did something else happen? I'm really confused here."

"So am I," Annie said.

"What's going on?" Cooper asked, walking up with T.J.

"What happened to you?" Kate asked T.J., sounding even more surprised than she had the first time.

Annie looked at T.J. She could see why Kate sounded so confused. T.J.'s eye was all black and blue, and his mouth was puffy. He had assorted scrapes on his cheek and chin.

"Will someone please tell me what's going on here?" Kate said in exasperation. "Who beat up T.J.?"

"The college guys," Annie said. "Well, one of them."

"Hey," T.J. said in protest. "I got him worse than he got me."

"And who came to your house?" Kate said, turning to Sasha.

"Social Services," she answered.

"Social Services came to your house?" said Cooper. "Why?"

Sasha held up her hands. "Time out," she said. "Rewind. Start over."

Everybody shut up and waited for her to speak. When she was sure they weren't going to interrupt her, she continued. "I'll let T.J. or Cooper or whoever fill you in on the college guy thing. *My* story is about Social Services. On Saturday afternoon this car shows up at our house. It was one of the guys from Thea's office."

"Thea's a social worker for the city," Cooper informed T.J., who nodded.

"This guy had two other people with him. Apparently, they're case investigators."

"What did they want?" asked Annie.

"To take me away," Sasha said flatly.

"What?" Cooper exclaimed. "Why?"

"Because of the letter my mom wrote to the paper," said Sasha. "This guy she works with read it and decided to use it as evidence that she's an unfit parent."

"Because she's a witch?" said T.J.

Kate nodded. "Tyler's dad tried to use that excuse when he and Tyler's mom divorced," she said.

"So what happened?" Annie asked Sasha.

Sasha sighed. "Lots of drama," she replied. "I guess this jerk has had it in for her for a long time because he thinks she's weird. He tried to get her fired when she put up a notice about one of the open rituals on the community bulletin board, and he makes all kinds of stupid comments about her being a witch."

"But those things aren't illegal," said Annie.

"Right," Sasha said. "There's nothing he can do about it. But this time he tried to convince these caseworkers that an 'admitted witch,' as he called her, should not be allowed to be the legal guardian of a minor. He called them and told them that Thea was doing all kinds of weird rituals and stuff with me in the house and insisted that they investigate."

"Man," Cooper said. "Thea must have gone nuts on him."

"Pretty much," said Sasha. "She really let him have it. She got up in his face and told him he had no business being there and that if he ever said so much as another single derogatory word about her or Wicca she was having him brought up on religious discrimination charges."

"What did the caseworkers say?" T.J. asked her.

"After they got Mom and this guy apart they came inside with us. They made him wait in the car and her wait in the kitchen. They talked to me for about an hour and asked me all kinds of dumb questions. Then they told Thea that everything seemed fine and that they weren't going to proceed with any kind of investigation, which was lucky for them, because I think she would have gone through the roof if they'd said anything else."

"Wow," Annie said. "First we get attacked and then this nut job tries to have you taken away from Thea. What a weekend. How was yours, Kate?"

"Okay," she said, not mentioning her visit to Dr. Hagen. "My parents pretty much left me alone."

"At least someone had a little bit of peace and quiet," commented Cooper.

"I'll tell you. I was really scared there for a while," Sasha said. "I finally find a home—with Wiccans—and then I almost get taken away from it just because somebody thinks being a witch means you can't take care of kids. Thea's the best mom I could ever hope for. That guy's just lucky I wasn't within kicking distance."

"I can't say the same for good old Todd," Cooper remarked, and Sasha grinned.

"Yeah," she said. "That *was* good."

"Are we all set for Greeley's class?" Cooper asked Annie.

Annie groaned. "As ready as we're going to be."

"We rehearsed a little bit over the weekend," Cooper told the others. "That is, when I wasn't fighting with my mother."

"What did *she* do?" Kate asked, thinking of her own currently rocky relationship with her own mother.

"Just being totally unsupportive," Cooper replied as the bell rang. "I'll fill you in later. See you in history."

They scattered to their various classes, but soon enough it was time for second period and Mrs. Greeley's history class. As soon as everyone was in the room and seated, Mrs. Greeley began.

"I hope the prosecution and the defense are both ready," she said, pulling out her desk chair and sitting down. "Why don't we have the accused come and sit in front of the class."

Cooper stood up and walked defiantly to the empty chair that Mrs. Greeley had positioned facing the rest of the students. She sat down and looked out at her classmates with a stony glare.

"Much as some of the first American colonists

were, Miss Rivers has been accused of exceeding the boundaries of free speech," Mrs. Greeley said. "Today we will hear arguments both for and against her actions. Then you, the jury, will vote to decide whether she is guilty or innocent. The prosecution will go first."

John Reynolds stood up and walked to the front of the room. He turned and smiled at the class. "Ladies and gentlemen of the jury," he said. "The defendant has been accused of exceeding the right to free speech as defined by our society, which in this case means the society of Beecher Falls High School. By wearing a symbol that some people find offensive and even threatening, she has created an atmosphere that interferes with the rights of others to attend school in a safe environment. That alone is reason enough to justify banning this particular symbol from being displayed."

He paused, walking behind Cooper's chair and standing there for a moment as if he were thinking about something. Then he put his hands on the back of the chair and leaned forward.

"Miss Rivers," he said. "Would you agree that all students should be able to come to school without worrying about feeling as if they are in danger?"

"Sure," Cooper said. "But I don't see how my necklace makes anyone feel unsafe."

"And would you agree that nobody should have to look at images they find offensive?"

"No," Cooper said. "I wouldn't agree with that.

I find Britney Spears's wardrobe offensive, but a third of the class has versions of it plastered all over their notebooks."

There was a wave of laughter from the other students, but Mrs. Greeley banged on her desk with her hand. "Order!" she barked.

"Let me rephrase that question," said John. "Would you agree that, for example, an African American student shouldn't have to come to school and see people walking around wearing white hoods?"

"That's a ridiculous example!" Cooper said, turning to look at John angrily. "Nobody would do that."

"But what if they did?" he said, holding up one finger. "Wouldn't they have the right to under the notion of free speech that you're advocating?"

"No," Cooper said. "White hoods would fall under the category of hate speech. I mean it's not speech, exactly, but they symbolize hate speech so it's sort of the same thing."

"And doesn't your necklace represent something?" said John. "Doesn't it represent certain beliefs and ideas that can be threatening to others?"

"Only if they don't understand it," Cooper shot back. "It doesn't represent anything hateful."

"Really?" said John. "Isn't it true that the pentagram is often used by so-called Satanists?"

"I don't know," Cooper said. "I'm not a Satanist."

John smiled indulgently. "Of course you're not,"

he said. "But the fact remains that the five-pointed star is often associated with Satanism, and many people who see you wearing it might not be as aware as you are. They might think that your necklace *does* indicate an interest on your part in Satanism. They might not know that you're really a, what do you call it, Wiccan?"

"Yes," Cooper said.

"They might not know that you're Wiccan," John continued. "Don't you think it's unfair to make them feel uncomfortable?"

"It's not my fault they're stupid," Cooper replied angrily. "Besides, I'm not the only one who wears this symbol. Lots of people in this school wear Marilyn Manson T-shirts, and those have pentagrams on them. Witchcraft symbols are also all over the *Blair Witch* stuff. Are you going to ban all of that, too?"

"That's a good question," John replied. "Maybe we should."

He turned to look at the class. "The fact is," he said, "this symbol does frighten many people. The purpose of school is to learn. It's not a place for espousing your personal beliefs and forcing other people to accept them. Her necklace is a distraction that prevents other people from fulfilling the purpose of coming to school, and as such it should be banned. This ban in no way interferes with Miss Rivers's own right to an education. It simply makes it easier for others to have that same right."

John returned to his desk, and Mrs. Greeley

looked at Annie. "Now the defense," she said.

Annie stood up and went to stand beside Cooper. She cleared her throat and began. "John's right," she said. "The purpose of school is to learn. But we don't just come here to learn about math and science and history. We come here to learn about each other. We have many different kinds of people at Beecher Falls High, people of different nationalities and backgrounds, people with different customs and beliefs. If we learn about these things, we learn about what makes people who they are.

"The symbol we're debating about today does represent something. It represents a way of thinking. If we try to 'protect' people from understanding what the pentagram means, we're basically saying that they're not smart enough to learn. You don't protect people by making choices for them. Sure, you might make them more comfortable, but you don't teach them anything. You don't give them the opportunity to grow."

Annie turned to Cooper. "You're a vegetarian, right?"

Cooper nodded. "Since I was twelve," she answered.

"How does it make you feel when you go through the lunch line and see hamburgers being served?" asked Annie.

Cooper shuddered. "It's disgusting," she said. "The way those cows are raised and killed is horrible."

"But you've never asked to have meat taken off

the menu?" said Annie.

"No," Cooper said. "If people want to poison their bodies with that garbage and contribute to the enslavement of animals that's their business."

Annie nodded. Then she turned to the class. "We have a lot of young women who attend Beecher Falls High," she said. "We walk through the halls every day. And sometimes when we do guys say stuff to us. They call us 'sweetie' or inform us that we 'look really hot.' Well, a lot of us don't like this. We also don't like looking at pictures of silicone-enhanced models that a lot of the guys tape to their locker doors."

All around the room, girls nodded their heads in agreement with Annie. Encouraged by this, she continued. "Maybe we should ban those kinds of pictures," she said, eliciting a series of boos and groans from some of the male students. "Maybe we should make it an offense to call a girl 'honey' or 'gorgeous.' To many of us that kind of talk is offensive and threatening."

She paused, letting her words sink in. She and Cooper had come up with a list of examples she could use in her argument. She'd already presented the first two, and it was time to use the last one.

"A lot of students are into sports," she said. "Many of you in this room are wearing clothes with team logos on them. Did you know that some people are trying to ban some of those logos because they're offensive? Think about it. The Washington

Redskins. Native American groups are highly offended by that image. The Atlanta Braves and their so-called tomahawk chop. It's a horribly racist image. But have these things been banned? No."

"But those are just fun," protested a boy in the back row. "It's *sports*."

Annie looked at Mrs. Greeley to see if she was going to comment on the outburst, but she was looking at Annie with a tight-lipped expression on her face. Annie knew the teacher was angry because she was hitting home with a lot of people.

"To *you* it's just sports," said Annie. "To other people they're images that perpetuate offensive stereotypes. So here's the question we need to answer: Why are some potentially offensive words and images protected while others aren't? Is it because they have to be offensive to the majority of people before they're considered really terrible? The necklace Cooper wears is being singled out simply because she's a minority. People don't understand what Wicca is. They don't want to take the time to understand it. So instead they try to get rid of it by banning its symbols. Is that right? I don't think so. We all have something that upsets us, whether it's seeing images of women portrayed as objects, hamburgers in the cafeteria, or necklaces that make us uneasy. If we banned everything that made people think, we'd be nothing but a school filled with mindless drones. So before you vote, think about this: Tomorrow something *you* think is important might be the next target."

She looked at Mrs. Greeley. "The defense rests."

Annie walked to her seat and sat down. Several students smiled at her and gave her thumbs-up signs. She noticed that John Reynolds wouldn't look at her.

"Okay," Mrs. Greeley said, standing. "You've heard both sides of the argument. Now it's up to you, the jury, to vote. Is Miss Rivers within her rights, or is she not? Please take a slip of paper and write guilty or innocent on it. Then we will collect them and I will count the votes."

For the next couple of minutes people ripped pieces of paper from their notebooks and wrote their votes on them. Then Mrs. Greeley walked around with a box and collected them all. When she had the last one she returned to her desk and dumped them out.

Annie watched as she opened the first vote and put it to one side. The next vote went into the same pile. But the third was set aside in a second pile. *I wonder which ones are which?* Annie thought.

She watched anxiously as Mrs. Greeley added slips to each pile. Annie tried to count them as she did, but she was too anxious. All she could do was watch each stack grow larger and larger. They seemed almost equal, but she couldn't be sure.

Finally, Mrs. Greeley opened the last slip and looked at it before tossing it into the pile to her left. Then she pushed all of the slips back into the box and looked up.

"Well," she said. "It was a very close vote. Apparently both counselors did a job of persuading some of you."

Annie's heart was racing. She wanted to win. She wanted to show up Mrs. Greeley, who, she knew, had set up the entire mock trial as a way of embarrassing Cooper. Annie looked at Cooper, who was still sitting in the chair, her arms folded across her chest.

Mrs. Greeley stood and walked over to Cooper. "As I said, the vote was very close," she said. "But your peers have found you guilty, Miss Rivers, by a vote of seventeen to twenty-two."

Annie's heart sank. How could that be? How could people be so narrow-minded? How could they actually fall for what John had said? But apparently they had. She looked over at John. He was looking back at her, a self-satisfied smirk on his face. In her chair, Cooper looked like she wanted to murder him. Annie looked at her friend sadly. *If we can't even convince the class*, she thought, *how are we ever going to convince the school board?*

CHAPTER 17

Cooper pushed her food around her plate. She wasn't hungry. She didn't even want to be eating dinner with her parents, but her father had insisted. In the five days that had passed since the incident with the college guys and her blow-up with her mother, she'd barely spoken to her mom. She hadn't told either of her parents about the humiliating "trial" in history class, or about the comments she faced daily from her fellow students. She hadn't told them that someone had written "witch" on her locker in black marker on Tuesday, or that T.J. had gotten into another fight when a guy in one of his classes had made fun of Cooper and T.J. had—once again—stood up for her.

At least he hasn't dumped you, she reminded herself. *Yet.* But Brian had dumped Annie, and Kate still wasn't being allowed to speak to Tyler. How long would T.J. keep putting up with her and the whole witch thing? He'd been the one to warn her about being too public, and now he was having to defend her because she hadn't listened. She appreciated it more than he probably knew, but would he keep doing it forever? Cooper didn't know. She'd hoped that everything would blow over quickly, but it just seemed to be intensifying. There had been more letters to the editor in the *Tribune*—mostly negative—and at class the night before Sophia had told her and Annie that people had been calling the store and accusing them of brainwashing the children of Beecher Falls.

Maybe you went too far this time, she told herself. *Maybe you should have listened to everybody*. She knew that if she had listened to T.J., and to her mother, she wouldn't be facing the horrifying prospect of standing in front of the school board again the next night. Her friends' lives wouldn't have been ruined. She could be looking forward to a night with the girls, or maybe jamming with T.J., instead of worrying about what was going to happen.

But even though she was miserable, and even though things were really rough, part of her just couldn't stop fighting. She knew that despite everything she was right. She did have the right to wear her pentacle, even if it made other people uncomfortable. She shouldn't have to hide her beliefs just because some people thought they were unusual. She shouldn't have to pretend she was someone else. The school board and the kids in her history class who had voted against her might not understand why it was important for her to wear the necklace, but they shouldn't be able to stop her from doing it.

But they have *stopped you*, she told herself. She wasn't allowed to wear the pentacle, and she was sure that after tomorrow she really wouldn't be able to. The school board, and especially Mr. Adams, would see to that. Sherrie had been running all over school for the past week, waving her petition around and getting more and more signatures. Every time Cooper saw somebody signing it she wanted to rip it out of their hands and tear it into hundreds of pieces. And once, when a guy had stopped her in the hall to sign it, Cooper had caught Sherrie looking at her with such an expression of triumph and sadistic pleasure that Cooper had had to go down to the music practice rooms and punch the soundproofed walls for half an hour to work out her frustrations.

"Are you coming to the school board hearing tomorrow?" Mr. Rivers asked his wife. He sounded uncomfortable, and he spoke to her almost as if she were a stranger instead of someone he'd been married to for nearly twenty years.

"I don't think that's a good idea," Mrs. Rivers answered, sounding equally uncomfortable. "I'm a teacher, Stephen. I'm not supposed to be taking sides here."

"You mean you're not supposed to be taking *my* side," Cooper said.

"No, that's not what I mean," said her mother. "Everybody already assumes that I'm taking your side because you're my daughter."

Cooper snorted. "I guess they don't know you very well, then, do they?"

Mrs. Rivers put down her fork. "For someone who talks a lot about freedom of speech, you need to learn to let other people have their opinions," she said.

Cooper looked down. She wanted to say something back, but she held her tongue. Once again, she wondered if maybe her mother was right. Was she so caught up in thinking that she had the right to wear her pentacle that she wasn't allowing herself to consider any other sides of the argument? She was the first to admit that she could be as stubborn as the day was long. Was she being stubborn now, or was she really in the right?

"You don't live in the real world, Cooper," her mother continued. "You don't have to deal with eight-year-olds asking you if your daughter can fly because their parents told them she was a witch. You don't have to go into the teachers' lounge for a cup of coffee and have people stop talking when you walk in."

"No," Cooper replied. "I just have to have people try to beat me up because I'm not ashamed of who I am."

"Which they wouldn't do if you'd just keep quiet!" her mother said, almost shouting.

"Can we not do this?" Mr. Rivers asked. "You two don't have to agree about this, but Cooper does have to go in front of the school board tomorrow. It would really help if everybody could remain calm, at least in our own house."

Cooper and her mother both looked at him. His face was strained, and for the first time Cooper realized how hard the situation must be for him. He was caught between his wife and his daughter, the two people he loved most in the world. He was fighting for a cause his wife didn't support, and he knew it.

The phone rang, shattering the unpleasant silence that had fallen over the table. *Great*, thought Cooper as she rose to get it. *It's probably someone calling with a bomb threat. That would be the perfect end to this day.*

She picked up the phone and said, "Hello?"

"Cooper," a woman's voice said. "It's Sophia."

"What's happened?" Cooper asked, worried. Sophia had never called her at home before. Had something awful happened at the store or, worse, to someone in the study group? Cooper knew she wouldn't be able to stand it if anything else bad happened.

"Nothing's happened," said Sophia. "At least, nothing bad. I think I have good news. Put your father on the phone."

"My father?" said Cooper.

"He's the one representing you tomorrow, right?" asked Sophia.

"Yes," Cooper answered.

"That's what I thought," said Sophia. "Put him on. This is important."

Cooper had no idea why Sophia would want to talk to her father, but she did as her teacher asked. As she walked into the dining room to get him she wondered what was going on. But she was going to have to wait to find out.

Over at her house, Kate was also eating dinner. Aunt Netty was telling them all about her day at the hospital.

"All my tests came back clear," she said. "The doctors are amazed."

"So you're cured, then?" asked Kate.

"I'm in remission," her aunt replied. "There's a chance the cancer will return. But right now everything looks fine."

"You can thank those new drugs they have," Mr. Morgan said, cutting his steak and taking a bite.

"At least partly," said Netty, looking at Kate and winking.

Kate knew that her aunt gave some of the credit for her recovery to positive thinking, and particularly to the ritual that Sophia and the others had done. While she didn't talk about it in front of Kate's parents, she'd told Kate privately that she'd felt something in her body change during the circle. She didn't know exactly what it was, but it had left her with a renewed sense of hope. She'd even, through Sophia, found a local coven near her own home and had met with them several times since her treatments for similar healing rituals. When Kate asked her if she had any interest in Wicca outside of the healing rituals, she'd smiled and said she didn't know. "But it's made me think about a lot of things," she'd added vaguely.

That was the only discussion about witchcraft that had taken place in the Morgan house. Kate's parents seemed relieved and happy that she'd liked Dr. Hagen and agreed to see her again, and they hadn't brought up the subject of Wicca at all since that first visit. Kate figured that they were hoping she'd forget all about it if nobody talked about it, so she gave them what they wanted and didn't mention a word about witchcraft or anything even remotely to do with it. She came home from school every day and stayed in her room, studying. She couldn't wait until the basketball league started the next week, because then at least she wouldn't feel trapped in the house.

But it also means you won't be going to class, she reminded herself. Not that she would be going anyway. Her parents would never let her do that, even if there had been a way to get out of the Tuesday night games, which there wasn't. She had already attended one meeting about basketball, and Coach Coleman had made it perfectly clear that she wouldn't be pleased with anyone missing any games. "Unless you're lying in a hospital bed or in a coffin, I expect you at all the games," she'd said.

"This may be intramural basketball, but for it to work everyone needs to show up."

Kate took *some* comfort in the fact that she'd at least be able to spend some time with Jessica and Tara. They were being incredibly supportive of her, and she was happy to have them back in her life. But what kind of life was it now that she didn't have the Tuesday night class, or the rituals with Annie and Cooper, to look forward to? What kind of life was it without Tyler?

Until it had all been taken away from her, she hadn't really realized just how important Wicca was to her. Before it had been something she enjoyed, but now that it had been forbidden she'd discovered that it had been so much more than that. She was still practicing her meditation and the things she could do alone in her room, but it just wasn't the same. She missed being with other people who were interested in witchcraft. She worried she would miss going to sabbat celebrations, with their songs and dances and costumes. Although she knew those things were only the outward trappings of the Craft, and that the real power and meaning lay in the mental and spiritual aspects of it, she still longed to have them back.

"We should go bowling tomorrow night," her father said suddenly, bringing her back to the conversation going on around her. "That would be fun. You used to love to bowl, Kate. Why don't we go out for pizza and a few games?"

Kate looked at her mother, who was smiling at her expectantly. She looked at her aunt, who was suddenly deeply intrigued by her dinner.

"Sure," she said. "That would be fun."

She knew that her father was trying to get her to do more things with the family. She'd overheard him telling her mother that he thought Kate's "problems" all started when they got too busy to do things with her. She'd wanted to tell him that wasn't true, but she couldn't. Now he was trying to make up for what he saw as a lack of parental involvement in her life. *My life has become an after-school movie*, she thought as she smiled at her parents.

The phone rang once. Kate tensed. It rang again, and she waited for a third ring. It didn't come, and the phone remained silent. Her mother said, "Must have been a wrong number."

Kate hurriedly took the last bite of her steak and stood up. "I've got a lot of homework to do," she said. "I'll be upstairs."

She dropped her dishes in the sink, ran water over them, and went upstairs, hoping no one would notice how much of a rush she was in. When she was in her room she went to her computer, logged online, and checked her E-mail. Sure enough, there was a message from Cooper. Their signal had worked.

She opened the mail and read it anxiously, wondering what news Cooper had for her.

**Big news from Sophia. You *have* to be at
the school board meeting tomorrow. Do whatever you need to. I'll explain more tomorrow.**

Short and to the point, Kate thought. But what did
Cooper mean? What kind of news could Sophia
have that would have any bearing on the school
board meeting? She couldn't wait to find out.

But there's no way you can go, she told herself. Her
parents would never let her near the meeting. In
fact, Kate was pretty sure her father had come up
with the bowling idea precisely to make sure she
didn't go. But Cooper said she had to be there. And
she *wanted* to be there. She wanted to support her
friend, and she wanted people to know that she
believed in something. But doing that would mean
defying her parents, and that would get her in even
more trouble than she was already in.

She sighed deeply. She was going to have to
make a choice, and she was going to have to make it
before seven o'clock the next night.

Annie sat in front of her altar, looking into the
flame of the white candle flickering in the dimness
of her bedroom. She'd been sitting there for some
time, trying to calm herself with her usual meditation
techniques. She'd already imagined herself in her
personal sacred space—a ring of towering redwood
trees. She'd imagined drawing power up from the
earth and letting it fill her body. She'd closed her eyes

and chanted the names of the goddesses she felt most close to: Freya, Hecate, Oya, Baba Yaga.

But she still felt unsettled. Things weren't going well, and for the first time since beginning her study of Wicca she was wondering if maybe it had been a mistake. Was everything that she and her friends were going through worth it? Two weeks ago she would never have thought she'd think so, but now she wasn't sure. T.J. had been roughed up, and the rest of them had narrowly escaped a similar fate. Sasha's living situation had been put in jeopardy. Kate was basically under house arrest by her parents. Cooper was the focus of a lot of fear and cruelty.

And she had lost a really great guy. The first guy she'd ever gone out with. The first guy she'd ever kissed. Gone. All because she'd written that editorial about being interested in Wicca.

If you'd just kept your mouth shut this wouldn't have happened, said the nagging voice that had been berating her all night.

The worst part about it was that she knew that what she and her friends were doing *was* right. If she was objective about it she could see that very clearly. Standing up for their rights was most definitely the thing to do. But why did doing the right thing have to be so hard? Why did it have to make them so unhappy?

There was a knock on her bedroom door, and her aunt said, "Can I come in?"

"Sure," Annie called out.

Aunt Sarah pushed the door open and came in.

"It's pretty in here with that candle going," she said.

Annie sighed. "I just wish I felt better," she replied.

Aunt Sarah came and sat down beside Annie. "I'm not invading sacred space or anything, am I?" she asked.

Annie smiled. "It's okay," she said. "I don't think the powers that be will mind. What's up?" Her aunt had never come up and interrupted one of her meditations before, so she knew something must be on her mind.

"I've been thinking about what you said at dinner tonight," said her aunt. "About feeling like this is too hard and that maybe you should just give up."

Annie didn't say anything. She wasn't sure what her aunt was getting at.

"When I was in college it was during apartheid in South Africa," Aunt Sarah continued. "A lot of us didn't support American commercial ventures in South Africa, as I'm sure you know."

Annie nodded. "There were lots of protests," she said.

"Right," Aunt Sarah said. "Well, at my school people were pretty apathetic. But there were still a lot of us who felt strongly about it. One day we decided to hold a protest. We marched downtown and took over an office building that was the corporate headquarters of a company largely invested in South Africa."

"Really?" said Annie, impressed. She'd never really thought of her aunt as the radical type.

"Oh, yes," said Aunt Sarah. "We had signs and chants and all of that."

"And what happened?" Annie asked her.

"They asked us to leave," answered her aunt. "When we wouldn't, they started yelling at us. Then the police came. But we still wouldn't leave. That's when they tear-gassed us."

"They did not," Annie said.

"They threw these containers of gas into the lobby full of people," Aunt Sarah said. "People started running and pushing. My eyes were burning so badly I couldn't see. I ended up getting knocked down. People were stepping on me and everyone was screaming. It was awful."

Aunt Sarah paused, as if she were experiencing all over again what it had felt like that day. "But even as I was lying on the ground with my eyes stinging, all I could think was, 'We're doing the right thing,'" she said. "I knew that apartheid was wrong and we were right, even if most people thought we were traitors, or cowards, or just plain crazy."

"Are you telling me I should buy a gas mask?" asked Annie.

Her aunt laughed. "No," she said. "I'm telling you that sometimes even when it feels like you've been knocked down one too many times it's still worth it.

Even if you don't win. We didn't win that day. Apartheid went on for years after that. But now when I look back on those days I realize that we really did make a difference, if only just a little bit. And even if we didn't change the world, we changed ourselves."

Annie looked at the candle flame again. Then she looked at her aunt. "Did you lose any boyfriends because of what you did?" she asked jokingly.

"Actually," her aunt said, "I met a great one at that protest. He helped me wash the gas out of my eyes and we ended up dating for almost a year."

Annie laughed. "So there's hope for me yet," she said.

Their conversation was interrupted by the ringing of the phone. A moment later Annie's little sister, Meg, yelled up the stairs, "Annie, it's Cooper. She says she has to talk to you."

CHAPTER 18

Cooper was nervous. It was 6:45. The school board meeting was going to begin any minute. Already the room was packed with people who had come to hear the proceedings. Both supporters and opponents of Cooper's petition were out in large numbers, and the room was filled with the sound of their sometimes heated discussions.

Cooper was seated in the first row of chairs, next to her father. A few rows behind her she saw T.J. sitting with Annie, her Aunt Sarah, and Meg. Kate wasn't there, but that was no surprise. She'd told Cooper she didn't know if she would be able to make it. Cooper would have liked to have her friend there, but she understood the situation Kate was in.

Actually, she understood it all too well. Her own mother had refused to come to the meeting. Cooper still felt hurt by her decision, but there was nothing that she could do about it. At least her father was there. And a lot of the members of both the Coven of the Green Wood and the coven that owned Crones' Circle were there. Archer, Julia, and some of the others were sitting halfway back with Tyler, Rowan, Thatcher, and a dozen other people Cooper didn't know. Apparently, word had gotten around in the pagan community and people had come out to lend their support to the cause.

But Sophia still wasn't there. That's what was troubling Cooper the most. Sophia should have been there already. She'd promised. A lot hinged on whether or not she came through.

"Relax," her father said, noticing her nervousness. "They'll get here."

Cooper turned around and sighed. "They'd better," she said, "or we're done for."

"Gee, thanks," Mr. Rivers said. "I didn't know I'd done such a bad job."

Cooper had to smile at her dad's pretend gloominess. "That's not what I meant," she said.

She looked around the room some more. "I can't believe all these people are here for this," she said.

"You've touched a nerve," said her father. "People feel very strongly about this issue, whether they're for it or against it. Face it, kiddo, you're a star."

"Yeah, well, I see one person who won't be getting an interview any time soon," said Cooper as she spied Amanda Barclay in the crowd. The reporter was busily taking notes as she talked to a pinched-face woman wearing a KEEP OUR SCHOOLS SAFE button. Cooper noticed with a little uneasiness that many people seemed to be sporting the buttons, certainly more than were wearing the pentacle-emblazoned pins being handed out by some of the local witches.

Cooper also noticed that Sherrie was making an appearance. She was sitting in the middle of the room, surrounded by a cluster of her friends. She saw Cooper looking at her and gave her a self-satisfied look. Cooper turned away. *I wish I could turn her into a toad*, she thought. *It would certainly be an improvement.*

The doors opened again and Cooper turned, hoping it was Sophia. But it wasn't. It was Mr. Dunford and the rest of the board. They had been waiting in another room so that they wouldn't be bothered by reporters or protesters. Now they made their way into the room and took their places behind the long table.

"Sophia's not here," Cooper said to her father. "Now what?"

"I think we all know why we're here," Mr. Dunford said. "So why don't we just get started. Miss Rivers, I've received the petition you filed and see that you indeed got the required number of signatures needed for us to review your case."

Mr. Dunford shuffled some papers around and picked up another piece of paper. "I have also received a petition from another student, Sherrie Adams, with a more or less equal number of signatures on it supporting our decision to ban your pentacle—and all occult symbols—from the school. Given that the student body seems to support our stance, have you come up with any reasons why we should reconsider?"

Cooper saw Mr. Adams look at Sherrie and smile. But Sherrie was the least of her problems at the moment. Sophia hadn't arrived and she was on her own.

"My daughter stands by the point we made last time," Mr. Rivers said, standing up. "Her wearing of a pentacle is an expression of her right to free speech. As you can see by the signatures on the petition, many of her schoolmates support her view."

"And many do not, Mr. Rivers," said Mr. Dunford, waving Sherrie's petition at him. "I must tell you that in all the years I've been on this board we have never once received a petition opposing another one. We have to take that into consideration. Clearly, a number of students are—as was expressed at our previous meeting—concerned that the appearance of occult symbols in the halls of Beecher Falls High School will be disruptive to their ability to attend school with a sense of comfort."

Cooper felt like getting up and running out. It was clear to her—more than clear—that the board had absolutely no intention of changing its mind. She felt as if she were sitting in Mrs. Greeley's history class again, watching as she counted the votes and knowing that her time was running out. They were going to lose, and it was only a matter of minutes before that was made official.

All of a sudden there was a commotion as the

doors to the room opened. Cooper turned to see Sophia sweep into the room. Behind her came a woman wearing a smart blue pants suit. Her blond hair hung to just below her shoulders, and she carried a brown leather briefcase.

Sophia rushed to the front and sat down next to Cooper. "Sorry we're late," she whispered. "Maggie's plane was late getting in from New York."

"Who are you?" asked Mr. Dunford, looking at the two women irritably.

"My name is Maggie Jerrold," said the blond woman.

"And what is your purpose here?" Mr. Dunford asked.

"Actually, I'm a lawyer," said Maggie. "I'm the senior legal counsel for the firm of Applegate, Whiting and Brisbey in New York."

Mr. Dunford looked at the other board members, all of whom appeared as confused as he was.

"I am also a witch," Maggie continued. "I have been for almost twenty years."

Cooper watched the looks on the faces of the board members change from confusion to utter shock. She knew they couldn't believe that the professional-looking woman standing in front of them was a witch.

"Are you here on some legal matter, Miss Jerrold?" asked Mr. Adams, looking at the lawyer as if he wished he could make her disappear. "Because this is not a legal proceeding."

"It's Ms. Jerrold," said Maggie. "And no, I'm not here on a legal matter, at least not yet."

She let her last words sink in as she opened her briefcase and removed some papers. Cooper could see the board members looking at one another uneasily as she did so.

Maggie turned around and faced the board again. "I understand that several people—including people on the board—suggested to Ms. Rivers that Wicca is not a legitimate religion."

"I believe what was said was that it is not recognized as a religion in the same way that other religions such as Judaism and Christianity are," said Mrs. Tracy coolly.

"I see," said Ms. Jerrold. "In that case, I would like to point you to the 1985 case of *Dettmer* vs. *Landon*. Mr. Dettmer was an inmate at the Powhatan Correctional Center in State Farm, Virginia. Prison officials repeatedly refused his request for candles, incense, statues, and other articles he required in order to practice his religion, which was Wicca. The excuse they used was the same one you appear to be using—that Wicca is somehow not as legitimate as other religions are. Well, the court saw differently. They ruled, and I quote, 'While there are certainly aspects of Wiccan philosophy that may strike most people as strange or incomprehensible, the mere fact that a belief may be unusual does not strip it of constitutional protection.'"

"Are you telling us that we should allow one of

our students to wear the symbols of a so-called religion just because a *convicted prisoner* was allowed to do so?" Mr. Adams asked.

"No, sir," answered Maggie. "I'm telling you that you should allow her to wear it because the right to freedom of religious expression is guaranteed under the First Amendment to the United States Constitution. Since Wicca is a legally recognized religion, I see no merit in the argument that you've been using to prevent Ms. Rivers from exercising these rights."

There was a stir in the audience as many people began to talk among themselves. A man in the back stood up. "Just because it's a religion doesn't mean it's *right*," he said.

"Please," Mr. Dunford said. "Let's keep this orderly."

"Ms. Jerrold," said Mrs. Reeder. "I can accept that Wicca is a religion under the law. But the fact remains that the symbol that Miss Rivers wants to wear is upsetting to a great number of students. Just look at all the names on this petition." She held up Sherrie's petition and waved it.

"I'm sure it is upsetting to a great number of people," replied the lawyer. "But Cooper still has the right to wear it."

"Not if we say she doesn't," said Mr. Alvarado. "I understand that neo-Nazis and Klansmen are allowed to hold demonstrations, but we don't allow them to parade through the halls of our schools in their uniforms."

"I'm not here to argue about the rights of those people," Maggie said. "But I can tell you that if Ms. Rivers so chooses she can take this matter to court. And I can also assure you that she will win. In March 1999 a student named Crystal Seifferly won just such a suit against the Lincoln Park School Board in Michigan. Like Ms. Rivers, Ms. Seifferly was asked to stop wearing a pentacle. Like you, the school board there attempted to equate the symbol with gang symbols and the symbols of Nazism and racial hate groups. However, the court ruled that the pentacle is a legitimate symbol of a recognized religious faith and as such cannot be banned."

Mr. Adams leaned back in his chair, glowering at Maggie Jerrold. He threw his pen on the table. The rest of the board members looked at one another. Ms. Chisolm and Professor Weingarten were smiling, but the others looked very unhappy.

"You can't let them do this, Marty!" yelled someone from the back as a number of other people seconded the declaration.

Mr. Dunford ran his hand over his mouth. "I don't see that we have a choice," he said. "If Ms. Jerrold's examples are legitimate—and I have no reason to think that they are not—then this could result in a very expensive legal battle for us. I don't think anybody wants that. So in light of all that we've heard here, I think we'll have to overrule ourselves and lift the ban."

Many people in the crowd began booing and hissing, but Cooper's supporters stood and began cheering. Some of them were hugging each other and laughing. Cooper's father looked at her and smiled. "We won," he said.

Suddenly, Cooper found herself standing up. "I want to say something," she said loudly.

The cheering and booing stopped as everyone looked at Cooper. She looked around the room at the expectant faces, then turned to face the school board.

"I never wanted this to turn into a legal thing," she said. "There's a law in Wicca that says that you should never force people to do something against their will. I know that doesn't exactly apply to this kind of situation, but I still think it's true. But if that's the only way to get you people to listen, then I guess I'll take it. I appreciate what Ms. Jerrold did here tonight. And I do think it's important that people understand that Wicca is a real religion and that Wiccans have the same right to wear the symbols of our faith as Christians and Jews and Muslims and everybody else does."

The room was silent. Cooper felt her heart pounding. She knew everyone was listening to her. She hadn't planned on saying anything, but now she knew that she had to keep talking. As she'd listened to Maggie Jerrold speak, she'd suddenly realized what the past few weeks had really been about for her.

"But when it comes down to it, this isn't about

laws. This is about people. I've taken a lot of grief for doing this. My friends have taken a lot of grief. Why? Because there are some of us who believe in something that the rest of you don't. Most of you don't know what it's like to have people try to beat you up because they think what you stand for is weird. You don't know what it's like to have people be afraid of you because you're different. Well, I feel bad for you people, because even though this has been one of the hardest things I've ever done, I've learned something really important.

"I don't need to be able to wear this pentacle to know that who and what I am is valid," she continued. "I know that anyway. I know because even though a lot of people have tried to stop me I've kept going. Before school started my friends and I did a ritual where I charged this pentacle with energy. I wore it hoping that it would help me face the challenges that came my way. Well, I have faced those challenges. But it wasn't the pentacle that helped me. It was the people in my life who supported me. Some of them are Wiccan and some of them aren't. But all of them respect me as a person, and they respect what I believe.

"I'll wear my pentacle," she said. "If that bothers some of you, that's your problem. But I'll wear it not to prove a point but because I'm *proud* to be Wiccan. I'm proud to be part of a group of people who care about me and who don't judge other people because of what they look like or what they believe. I'm proud to say that this is who I am."

She stopped talking and looked at the people looking back at her. Some of them were nodding their heads in approval. Others were most definitely scowling at her. *I don't care*, she thought suddenly. *I don't care what they think. This isn't about them. It's about me.* She felt happy, happier than she had in a long, long time. She didn't need anyone's approval or anyone's permission.

"I'm proud to be Wiccan, too."

Cooper looked up and saw Annie standing beside her aunt. She was looking at Cooper and smiling. Cooper smiled back.

"I'm proud, too," said Sophia, standing up so that everyone could see her.

"Me, too," chimed in Tyler, who was quickly followed by Rowan and several members of their coven, all of whom stood together, holding hands.

All around the room people stood up and said, "I'm proud to be Wiccan, too." Cooper watched them. Many she knew, but many she didn't. She looked at the different faces, each of them looking at her with pride. There were probably forty people standing, while the rest of the crowd looked at them.

"I'm proud to be Wiccan, too," said a quiet voice.

Cooper looked to see who had spoken and saw Kate pushing her way to the front of the room.

Oh, Goddess, she thought as she watched her friend come to stand beside Annie. *You are in such trouble now.* But Kate was smiling as she stood there, surrounded by many of her family's friends and neighbors, people who were sure to tell the Morgans what their daughter had done.

Cooper turned back around and looked at the board members. Many of them were looking down at the table, but some were watching her with a new respect. Mr. Adams, though, looked like he was about to burst. Looking at him, Cooper let out a satisfied laugh.

Maggie Jerrold came to stand beside her, putting her arm around Cooper. "Good work," she whispered in her ear. "They're never going to forget this for as long as they live."

Cooper looked around, taking in the people standing with her. There were a lot of issues that hadn't been resolved yet, and she knew that difficult challenges still awaited her. But for now she was happy, and she knew that when she needed strength she could remember this moment and remember what it felt like to win on her own terms.

"Neither will I," she said to Maggie. "Neither will I."

follow the
circle of three

with book 9:
through the veil

Annie stood on the street, looking up at the house in front of her. The street lamp beside her cast a warm pool of light around her feet, which were bare, and the cold night air chilled her skin. She rubbed her arms, shivering. *Why am I outside?* she wondered.

Fire! Annie thought. *That house is on fire!*

Then she knew where she was and why the house was so familiar to her. It wasn't just any house. It was *her* house. Not the house she lived in now in Beecher Falls with her Aunt Sarah and her younger sister, Meg, but the house she had lived in when she was a little girl. It was her house, and it was burning.

Not again, she thought, fear overcoming her as she realized what was happening. *Not again*.

She tried to move, but her feet wouldn't carry her forward. All she could do was watch as the flames in the window grew brighter. She wanted to scream, to call for help, but her voice was frozen inside of her. She knew that behind the window she was lying on the couch, where she'd fallen asleep after sneaking downstairs to plug in the Christmas tree lights and watch them twinkle. And she knew that her parents and Meg were still asleep upstairs, oblivious to the danger that was creeping toward them as the flames spread quickly through the house.

But now she had a chance to save her whole family. She knew that. All she had to do was run into the house. All she had to do was get her feet to move. She could find them and lead them to safety. They wouldn't have to die because of her.

She tried to move forward, but she couldn't. She was frozen, helpless, as she watched her house burn with her parents inside of it. No matter how much she tried to will herself forward her body wouldn't obey her. Something was holding her back.

She woke up then, knowing instantly that the dream was over. That was how it always ended. But she hadn't had the dream in almost three years. Why had it come back now?